DAVID

Cannon Fodder

VINTAGE BOOKS
London

Published by Vintage 2006

2 4 6 8 10 9 7 5 3 1

The author gratefully acknowledges the support of the
Arts Council of Great Britain whilst writing this book

First published in Great Britain in 2005 by
Secker & Warburg

Vintage
Random House, 20 Vauxhall Bridge Road,
London SW1V 2SA

Random House Australia (Pty) Limited
20 Alfred Street, Milsons Point, Sydney,
New South Wales 2061, Australia

Random House New Zealand Limited
18 Poland Road, Glenfield, Auckland 10, New Zealand

Random House (Pty) Limited
Isle of Houghton, Corner of Boundary Road & Carse O'Gowrie,
Houghton, 2198, South Africa

Random House Publishers India Private Limited
301 World Trade Tower, Hotel Intercontinental Grand Complex,
Barakhamba Lane, New Delhi 110 001, India

The Random House Group Limited Reg. No. 954009
www.randomhouse.co.uk/vintage

A CIP catalogue record for this book
is available from the British Library

ISBN 9780099478232 (from Jan 2007)
ISBN 0099478234

Papers used by Random House are natural,
recyclable products made from wood grown in
sustainable forests. The manufacturing processes
conform to the environmental regulations of the
country of origin

Printed and bound in Great Britain by
Bookmarque Ltd, Croydon, Surrey

contents

CANNON FODDER

Born in West Sussex in 1970, David L. Hayles
lives in London. He is the author of *The Suicide
Kit*.

ALSO BY DAVID L. HAYLES

The Suicide Kit

the process

It was time. My supervisor, Mr Godey, knocked on the
door and told me as much. Just as I was getting to quite
enjoy it here. I thought, I could go on living like this . . .
but I'd known my time was coming. I'd been eating well,
sleeping well. Sleeping ten hours a night, no dreams. My
room might have been something out of a moderately
priced hotel – bed, desk, chair, small bathroom (that itself
was an improvement on the bedsitter I'd ended up in,
before I'd come here, where I had to share a bathroom and
toilet down the hall). The window looked out on to the
enclosed courtyard in the centre of the complex.

Even though I didn't do much of anything during the
day, I was always tired by the end of it. I would sit in the
courtyard, or read a book in the small library. Maybe a
conversation with one of the others. I'd struck up a

friendship with two of the men there – the women were in a different block. One of them was a black fellow, Mitchell. He was quite young, big and anxious. He was very pensive and seldom spoke much – when he did, he was almost whispering. He never said why he was there – he'd just talk about his family, his wife and three boys. The other, Carpenter, was in his sixties, and seemed unconcerned about the whole set-up. The three of us, we'd sit and talk about anything, but not about *that* – Carpenter used to try and make jokes about it but we didn't encourage him. Some days, Carpenter would sit alone in the courtyard and play himself at chess.

I was quite happy there, doing nothing. Waiting for lunchtime, or dinner. I had breakfast in my room – a cup of coffee, orange juice, a couple of pieces of toast, buttered. Lunch and dinner I'd take in the dining room with Carpenter and Mitchell. Sometimes in the evening we'd drink a glass of wine. Carpenter would regale us with stories about a long string of ill-fated inventions he'd devoted his time and money to – the reason he was in this predicament. He claimed he'd invented, among other things, a beach ball with paddles, a magic cork and a miracle hair dye. The investment in the inventions, the cost of the patents, and the fact that none of them worked, had been his downfall. My own story wasn't as colourful.

One day ran into the next. I was given regular check-ups – weighed, measured, my blood tested – and some luxury – massage, steam rooms, things I had been unaccustomed to before.

Before, the days had gone so murderously slow, but the end of each month, well, *that* came around fast, without fail. It seemed like there was never a day when the rent wasn't due, when the bills on the cards and the loans and everything weren't due, half of them *overdue*, when there wasn't going to be that knock at the door.

I'd spend every waking hour (which was most of the time, I didn't sleep much) thinking about money: what I owed, how to pay it, how to get it. What I didn't have but needed. When you don't have work you have plenty of time to think about it, to dwell upon it, to despair about it. Mainly despair. I'd think, well, I'll take a walk, try and clear my head a little, but you take a step or two and think – too many more of those, buster, and you'll wear out your shoes and then you'll need a new pair, and how will you pay for them? I'd think, well, at least it's summer, I can enjoy the sun, then I'd think – soon it will be winter, and I'll have to turn on the electric heater, and that will be more bills! I couldn't do anything, not a damn thing. Come out for a drink, come out for a meal, people'd say, take your mind off it – only it wouldn't, it would put my mind on it; I'd sit there and think, I can't afford this, not a single mouthful, not one sip, and I couldn't enjoy it for a second and they'd say 'I'll pay, don't worry about it,' and that'd

3

only make me feel worse. The invitations dried up pretty soon, and it wasn't hard to see why. The phone calls dried up full stop, not surprising when you no longer have a phone to receive them on. I was pleased when the phone was disconnected – it meant an end to those constant, bullying calls from the bank, demanding overdue repayments in that sneering, supercilious tone. Those had really made my day.

Some days I'd come up with a brand new plan, but that glimmer of hope didn't last long. Every day the penury, the debt stacking up a little bit more, moment by moment . . . how had I let it come to this, how would I get out of it? Could I ever? It was maddening, my mind going round in circles, no solution offering itself, but the debt sat there, quite happy, smug, fattening itself, with no effort on its part, me feeding it every day without fail – it certainly had a healthy appetite, while I grew thin with worry; the end of the month creeping silently closer. My hair had started falling out, but at least that was some sort of progress.

Of course, I'd tried the bank.

'Mr Freeman, until you make good on the previous loan –'

'Yes, well, you see, the situation is – I need money to get going again, and then – the thing is . . .'

'Get going *again*?'

'To generate business –'

'Business?'

'That's right – it was going quite well until –'

'From what I can see it wasn't going well at all.'

'Small businesses – they take time – I'm sure, as you know –'

'The bank can't extend a further loan, Mr Freeman.'

'How can I pay the loan back without –'

'Perhaps your wife could –?'

'Ex-wife.'

'I see, yes. Have you got any dependants?'

'No.'

'Any family who could support you?'

I shook my head. 'They – they've done all they can.'

'And I'm afraid so have we, Mr Freeman, I'm afraid so have we.'

I'd tried to make a go of it, I really had. Go for it!, while you still have a chance, she'd said. She'd goaded me into doing it, didn't let up about it, quality of life she said. Fortune favours the brave, right? THINK BIG! And hell, the bank near begged me to take the loan. It was all smiles at the start and wishing me good luck . . . and look where that got me. I didn't have a sou left in the account before I'd so much as said 'open for business'. Funny how quickly the bills mount up when you're into those minus figures. Like vultures circling a dying animal, ready to swoop down. I was all alone in that thing, with a debt hanging over me that I had no way of clearing. She'd helped me get into debt, but she sure as hell wasn't around to help me get out of it. She'd left in a hurry, but not without a parting shot. 'And to cap it all,' she'd said, 'you're going bald!' I could have done without that.

My only other option was to go back to work. But who'd have me? Not the old job — and not because of pride either — they'd laugh me right out of there. Oh sure, I'd been offered some work. By my calculations, on that wage, I'd be close to retirement before I'd even made a dent in paying back the debt. As for something decent — it wasn't going to happen. I could have declared myself bankrupt. Then I'd be in hock to my creditors from here until doomsday. What kind of miserable existence would that have been? There had to be another way. I kept thinking something would come up.

It did. Sort of.

I didn't figure it was junk mail at the time, but sure enough, it was — a cheap trick sticking it into a brown envelope with a handwritten address like that. But it wasn't like all the other offers posted through the door every day — with a crummy photo-story showing the release from debt, from that hideous purgatory, just one phone call and it's all smiles and happy families, or the picture of some smiling mug fanning wads of notes out at you, currency hanging out of his pockets; the simple 'repayment plan' chart. Everyone knew the score with those, the last refuge of the desperate man. You'd sign up for a loan that cleared all your debts – bank, credit card, store cards, everything – in one fell swoop. At last, sleep easy. Then *they* started sending *their* bill. The advantage being it was only the one bill to settle each month – you knew what was coming and when – no hassle! But you were in a deeper hole than before. So, what do you know, you can't even make that payment, they send round the boys with baseball bats to lean on you a little. Take out another loan to clear the first loan, et cetera, et cetera, et cetera. Now, I was stupid, but I wasn't dumb. I could understand why people went for it. Money worry – it's about the worst one there is.

But as I said, this one looked different from the others. Just six words, and a number.

CLEAR YOUR DEBTS. NOTHING TO PAY.

There was no easy way out, I knew that. I mean to say, I was resigned to that.

There was no harm in phoning, though. At the first hint of some kind of scam, some kind of con trick – which it would inevitably be – I would hang up. I dialled on a payphone with a prefix so they couldn't phone me back and try and push me into signing up for some heavy loan. No harm in it.

*

7

The interview had been arranged for the following morning. I was anxious, naturally, anxious to get it over with. I was expecting my hopes to be dashed so there hadn't been any point prolonging it. But, they had said, it was only a preliminary interview; if, at any point, either client or adviser did not wish to proceed then the process would go no further. That's what they'd called it – 'process'. Not loan; not transaction – *process*.

I looked at myself in the mirror before I set off, the living, breathing deficit. I appeared a little shabby, with a button missing from my jacket and my trousers could probably have done with a dry-clean, but they were dark so it didn't show. Regret to report, more scalp visible than usual. Probably better not to look spick and span though – that might give the wrong impression. What I wanted to suggest was that I really could use some financial help. I think I fitted the bill.

By the time I got to the address I was sweating. It was a big glass building in the business district. No sign, but the number was right. I waited outside for a bit to cool off, but I needn't have worried. As soon as I went through the glass doors I was hit with a cold blast by the air conditioning.

The receptionist told me to sit and wait until I was called. The place was like a high-class bank; the carpets spotless, immaculate polished surfaces – the sort of environment that inspired confidence, trust if you like. The receptionist was very still, unfussed, and when the phone rang you could barely hear it. She spoke quietly into the receiver.

There was a jug of iced water on the low table in front of me. I poured a glass and noticed that my hand was trembling.

'Mr Freeman?'

A short man in a grey suit, with neatly trimmed black hair and wire-framed glasses, had appeared as if from nowhere, and was standing over me.

I put the glass down, stood up and extended my hand. He shook it briefly.

'I'm Donald Brockbank, your debt re-coordinator.'

'Pleased to meet you.'

'First of all, Mr Freeman, we're going to need you to submit to a medical. Company policy.'

'Medical?'

'We don't want you dropping down dead on us, now do we?'

'Quite.'

'Strictly a formality. The nurse will show you through,' he said, gesturing towards a young woman in a pressed white uniform, waiting by a door to one side of the reception area.

'I'll see you directly,' he said.

Brockbank was reading a file on his desk when I went in. He motioned for me to sit down.

Brockbank's office was modest, clean, unintimidating.

'Yes, it all seems to be in order . . . your medical, I mean. I think we're ready to proceed. If that is all right with you, Mr Freeman.'

'Oh, absolutely,' I said. I felt quite, quite relaxed, relieved that I'd passed the medical so painlessly. The nurse had put me at ease with her gentle, calming manner. We'd even had something of a conversation during the procedure. I realised then that for an hour or more I hadn't thought about money, the debt, anything, for the first time in . . . we'd just talked, and it had been pleasant.

'So – how does this work?' I said, leaning forward.

'Well,' Brockback said. 'We clear your debt –'

'You clear everything?'

'Everything.'

'I see. And in order to do that – I –'

'Well, we'll come to that. Now what I need you to do is bring in all your records of outstanding loans, your bank details, and so forth – everything really – and we'll take it from there. We'll arrange a meeting.'

'And that's it?'

'For now. One more thing, Mr Freeman.'

'What's that?'

'Discretion.'

'Discretion?'

'You've been specially selected, Mr Freeman. This is

not a service we offer to all and sundry. Nor would we want to. Any more than you would want to broadcast your financial trouble.'

'I see, yes.'

'Discretion works both ways,' he said.

He stood up and straightened his tie.

'It's been nice to meet you, Mr Freeman,' he said, shaking my hand.

'Thank you,' I'd said, and left the office.

On the way home I took a walk through the park. I stopped and took it all in. It was like something had been lifted.

A few days later a letter arrived with details of my next meeting. I went along.

'What happened to Mr Brockbank?'

'Mr Brockbank?'

'My debt coordinator.'

'Re-coordinator. Your case has been reassigned to me. Normal procedure. Colin Jessup.'

Jessup was tall and thin, and not a hair out of place.

'Pleased to meet you. I've brought —'

'Yes, now, this is everything?'

I nodded.

'Hmm. Well. Given this, and the medical, I think we can work something out,' he said.

I couldn't be sure if what I was feeling was a feeling of elation. It had been a long time since I'd felt that.

'A relief, eh?' Jessup said.

'I should say.'

'Well, don't worry. Everything's in hand. Now, let me tell you about the process.'

He told me.

I listened.

'And all you have to do is sign, Mr Freeman, and leave the rest to us.'

I didn't make my decision there and then. They told me I could take as long as I liked. And in the meantime, I could stay, undisturbed, in moderate comfort, in their facilities, the idea being that I would be on, effectively, neutral territory, not back in my predicament where I might feel *forced* into making a decision. I took them up on their offer.

And so my stay began. There wasn't a great deal to do, but I got used to *that*.

And I got to thinking – what kind of life did I have anyway – had I *had*? One disappointment after another. And the last few years – Jesus, that was no way for anyone to live. Once you've lived a certain way, to have one's circumstances reduced – *unaccustomed as we are . . .*

I made my mind up pretty soon.

All I had to do was sign the paper.

And that was it.

*

I was moved to new quarters, which is where I was allowed to mix with the others, where I met Carpenter and Mitchell, and my stay proper began. A tag was put on my ankle, a prerequisite that prevented us from leaving. From what I'd been told that was not an option anyway; the place was secure, the courtyard the only outside view we had. We were allowed to move freely within the place and one evening, after I'd settled in, I went for a look around. Not that there was a great deal to see – the long white corridors, the floors polished to a high shine, illuminated with yellowish fluorescent strip lighting, were empty, seemingly devoid of doors to the outside. I saw the occasional attendant, who would nod almost imperceptibly. Soon I'd walked all the way around, and was back at my door.

Godey had paid me a visit in my room. Godey was a reassuring presence – mid-fifties, quite short, soberly dressed in a grey suit, a pale blue shirt and tie, black oxfords.

'How are you, Mr Freeman?' he asked in his usual cheerful manner. His round, quietly friendly face, hinting at benevolence, made you forget what you were there for.

'Fine,' I told him – as a matter of fact. I really did feel as well as I ever had. Relaxed. What the hell did they put in that food?

'Then that is good. Mr Freeman, uhm, as part of all this, and I'm sure one of the others will have mentioned it to you, we have a "screening process". For our clients. For them to get to see you. If, and when, you're chosen, things will move along pretty swiftly afterwards.'

'Yes, Carpenter did mention it.'

'You'll have your first this afternoon. There's nothing to it. The nurse will call you.'

I nodded.

'Good, good,' he said, and went out.

We were lined up against a wall in a long white room. Twelve of us. Stripped naked, standing there, waiting. No one spoke.

A door opened at the end of the room.

We were called to screenings quite frequently. Carpenter was always in a jovial mood. 'They won't want someone like me,' he'd say to me as we were walked along towards the room. 'Not me, past my sell-by date! But him – they'll want him!' he said, jerking a thumb towards Mitchell, walking ahead of us. 'I'm surprised he hasn't been taken yet.'

And sure enough, it came to pass, some weeks later. An elegant-looking lady stepped into the screening room, being led along by a small dog on an expensive leash. She moved along the row, looking us up and down, the dog sniffing at our feet.

She paused, and pointed at Mitchell, then turned and walked out, the dog trotting along behind her. Mitchell was led away by the attendants, his head bowed. That was the last we saw of him.

We were sent back to our rooms.

It had started to snow. The courtyard was covered in a bright white blanket of the stuff. Christmas soon. Carpenter told me he had once invented a fake Christmas tree that shed plastic pine needles. 'What was the point of that?' I asked him. He scratched his chin for a moment. 'I'm not quite sure myself, now I come to think of it,' he said. Christmas! Ha! It didn't mean anything to us at all.

We were called to another screening. It was the same procedure as before.

After five minutes of standing there, the door at the end of the room clattered open.

'Here they are, here they are!' a voice boomed. A man wearing sunglasses and a dark suit entered. He was about five foot tall, fat like a beachball, bald but with wisps of grey hair. He waddled forward, with Godey behind him. Two other men stepped in and stood flanking the door.

The fat man started along the row.

He stopped three along, slapped his hands together, grinned, and reached to massage the man's shoulders. 'Hmm, good, good.'

He worked his way slowly down the row, coming towards me and Carpenter. Carpenter was whistling to himself. The man stood in front of me and he narrowed his eyes and inspected me closely. I could smell whisky on his breath. '*This* one –' he said, stepping to one side in front of Carpenter. Carpenter did a double take. 'Wha – no –'

'Yes, this one,' he said, prodding Carpenter's wrinkled, sagging shoulder.

The attendants grabbed hold of Carpenter. He struggled as best as he could for a bit, then went limp in their hold and they took him out.

A few days later I spotted his chess set on the wall in the courtyard. I packed it up and took it back to my room. I missed Carpenter and his ridiculous stories about his failed inventions. He said the last thing he'd invented was a hair thickener and that I could have used some of it. I began to think I wouldn't care if I was chosen. I didn't have to wait too long to find out.

After the screening they took me back to my room to wait.

*

Mr Godey came into my room.

'Just came to say goodbye,' he said, and shook my hand. 'The nurse will call you.'

Then he left.

I was strapped down and was being wheeled through. I felt woozy. The nurse was looking down at me.

I could hear the wheels of the trolley, but they sounded a million miles away, whirring along the polished white floor as if on another planet, the strip lights flashing overhead like stars passing by. So this was how it was supposed to be.

The trolley banged through swing doors into darkness.

'Here we are . . .'

I felt the words but couldn't hear them.

The nurse leaned in close to my neck.

Coldness spread through my shoulder, up the side of my skull. I

*

The man in the white coat and gloves looked down at the trolley and noted hair loss. Funny, he thought, hair loss was always endemic in these cases. It didn't matter anyway, they wouldn't be needing the hair. They always shaved the entire body. He took out the clippers and went to work.

you can be a writer!

WHY NOT BE A WRITER?

You could earn money from writing books, articles, short stories and even radio plays. Our course has helped thousands get their name in print and make a living from WRITING. With a series of simple exercises and our world-renowned 'postal tutorials', you'll soon be able to make CASH from your writing skills.

'After doing your course I now earn twice as much from writing than from my proper job!' T. Bennet, Lancs

'I did your course and now I write bestsellers!' J. Moule, Suffolk

'I never would have had a clue about writing without your course, thanks.' T. Parsons, London

Send now for your free introductory pack.

Dear Sir
    Please send me my free introductory pack.
Yours
Mr C. Tupper

Dear C Tupper
Enclosed is your free introductory pack. When you decide to enrol, simply fill out the form on the back of the leaflet, complete the short exercise and send it with a cheque for the full amount to the address at the bottom of the form. And here's wishing you luck with your new career in WRITING.

Dear Sir
    Enclosed is my registration fee and the short-story exercise on 'Something that has happened to me'.
Yours
C. Tupper

Dear C Tupper
Thank you for enrolling with the Writers' Gold Medal Literature Masterclass Accreditation Course.

Your short-story piece 'A Day in the Life of C. Tupper', although very readable, lacked the 'sellability' necessary to earn a living as a WRITER. Editors look for stories that are UNUSUAL – EXCITING – GRIPPING. Try again, and this time think of something that has happened to you that will surprise the reader and make them want to read on. You can always 'embellish' the story to make it more interesting.

Good luck.

Dear Sir

Enclosed is my short story based on a true-life experience.

Yours

C. Tupper

Dear C Tupper

Re your 'short story'; although we agree that a flat tyre on the motorway was an 'unexpected' and 'surprising' incident for you, it may not be so much so for the person reading it. Have another go, and this time really think of something that will grip the reader.

Dear Sir

Here is another short story, this time about getting locked in the office at work by accident.

Yours

C. Tupper

you can be a writer!

Dear C Tupper
We do feel you are getting there, but aren't quite there yet. Don't give up! Have another crack at it! There might be something staring you in the face you haven't thought about using for material as a short story.

Dear Sir
    Here is another true-life story with all the requisite 'ingredients'.
Yours
C. Tupper

Dear C Tupper
Enclosed are our notes on your short story.

C Tupper: 'Short Story'
Tutorial One: Overview

- The story holds the attention but suggest changing from first person to third person so the reader can be objective.
- 'I done not a thing like this before' should read: *He'd never done anything like this before.*
- When you say the narrator hears the TV from the next-door neighbours' and wonders if they have heard what *he's* been doing, why not describe *what* he hears, i.e. – 'He heard the theme tune to *Heartbeat* from next door' for example, or even *Coronation Street*.

Dear Sir

Enclosed is my short story reworked.

Yours

C. Tupper

C Tupper: 'Short Story'
Tutorial Two: Methodology

- Make more of the 'nosy neighbour' character to heighten the tension.
- Similarly, in the description 'He imagined he was back at school in pottery class making a clay ashtray, and squeezed'. How about *'She felt like putty in his hands'*?
- Try and think of a catchy title to really 'sell' the piece.

These are only suggestions.

Dear Sir

I have made the adjustments as suggested – I'm really getting the hang of this.

Yours

C. Tupper

PS – new title added

PPS – the 'nosy neighbour' only came to the door once (should I embellish?)

C Tupper: 'Dial M for Mercy'
Tutorial Three: Grammar

- 'He feeled a sense of relief' should be 'He felt a sense of relief'.
- Instead of saying 'her eyes bulged like two grapefruits on a moonlit night', why not like 'two hard-boiled eggs' instead?
- Remove extraneous exclamation marks (e.g – '"Help!!!" she screamed out').

Dear Sir

  I have removed most of the exclamation marks!!! (joke).

Yours

C. Tupper

C Tupper: 'Dial M for Mercy'
Tutorial Four: Fine-Tuning

Keep it simple:
- 'After cutting up the body he washed his hands thoroughly until they were clean' is a tautology – *'He washed his hands thoroughly'* is enough.
- 'He ran round the house in a blind panic looking for bin bags to put the body into, like as if he was late for a plane and had gone to the wrong terminal, and the next flight wouldn't be until tomorrow and by then it would be too late.' 'He ran around the house in a blind panic' would suffice.

- The disposal of the body is frankly implausible, and strains the credibility of the story. Rework this.
- And finally, why does he strangle her in the first place? – surely not simply because of a row over her smoking in the house?
- Also, what will he tell his neighbours if they ask after his wife?

Dear Sir

Enclosed 'Dial M for Mercy' with the changes made. I hope it is up to scratch. As far as point iii) goes, yes, that was exactly how I disposed of the body, and iv), yes, it was because of a row over smoking inside the house (crazy isn't it? I guess something inside me just snapped).

Yours

C. Tupper

PS – I told the neighbours she'd gone to stay at Lee on Sea with her nan.

Dear C Tupper

Congratulations! You have now completed the Writers' Gold Medal Literature Masterclass Accreditation Course. Send now for a list of magazine and publication contacts with which to place your short story. Remember, if you don't get a story placed within six months, your course fee will be refunded.

Good luck!

you can be a writer!

Dear Sir

Enclosed is a 'short story', 'Dial M For Mercy', that I thought you might feel suitable for inclusion in *Readers' Quarterly*. I recently completed the Writers' Gold Medal Literature Masterclass Accreditation Course. It is 'based on a true story'(!). I hope you can use it, and look forward to hearing from you.
Yours
C. Tupper

Dear Mr Tupper
Never write to this address again.
Submissions Editor, *Readers' Quarterly*

Dear Sir
None of my work has been published within the six-month period stipulated in the bumpf. Please refund my course fees.
Yours
C. Tupper

FAO C Tupper
Enclosed: course refund less administration costs

Dear Sir

Please send me the free introductory pack on 'Becoming a cartoonist'. There are some really funny goings-on here that I think will give me lots of material to become a cartooner. Plus I'll have plenty of time to practise, at Her Majesty's pleasure!!

Yours

C. Tupper

savage incidents at the college reunion

I never wanted to go to no reunion, why would I? I never kept in touch with anyone, I didn't even finish my course, that bloody place made my life a misery, or at least the people there did. Bloody bastards, most of them. But they keep in touch with me, the college that is, sending me leaflets and that, asking for money for tennis courts and stuff, donations and whatnot, and I thought, well, why couldn't we have had tennis courts when I was there, why should I give money, they'd be no good to me now (not that I play tennis, I'm not good at sport or anything). And I keep getting that bloody *Alumni News* pamphlet through the post, and sometimes I flick through it on the bog, God knows why, read about how so-and-so is doing this and going round the world and so-and-so is starting a new business and so-and-so is married with two lovely kids, etc. It's bloody crap.

And now this, a Graduates' Reunion, bloody leaflet inviting me to a 'special alumni reunion, a barbecue-style dinner followed by a disco in a marquee in the main quadrangle'. The theme is to *dress as your favourite Hollywood star,* or black tie. Bollocks. I wish they'd stop sending me this stuff. The tickets are bloody expensive as well.

I decided to go to the reunion after all. It was partly because of the film theme, I'm well into my films, people'd know that if anyone ever took the time to ask. I took a couple of days off from the video shop and took the train up there in the afternoon. It started about eight o'clock. Doing that journey reminded me of going back to college after the holidays. All the posh-nobs turning up in their cars driven by mummy, me lugging my rucksack up the hill to the campus and them tearing past beeping their horns and shouting out the window at me but never stopping to give me a lift. Even my first-year room-mate, going flying past and giving me the finger out the window. He was a proper bastard, bringing girls back to the room and that, bringing his mates back, using my stuff. One time he says, we're going to have a party in the room, is that all right? I said, I suppose so, I'll invite some people, and he says, what are you talking about, I want you to make yourself scarce. What a bastard.

I wore my 'fancy dress' outfit on the train, no one really noticed or said anything, it wasn't that out of the normal. I wondered how many people would dress up. Probably quite a lot of them to make a right show of themselves and go on about how brilliant they were doing. If they asked me what I was doing I'd just say, 'I work in a video shop. Assistant manager.' So what? It's not that bad and you get to watch films all day, only during the day you have to put on U, PG, maybe 12 certificate ones because there are kids around. Once I put on *Scanners* with the head exploding bit and got into right trouble because a kid was there and his mum came in later and complained to the manager and said her boy'd got nightmares after that and he had to give her free rentals for a month. The manager said to me, 'Put on *Harry Potter*, but don't put on bloody *Scanners*.' Point taken, I didn't want to lose my job, it's bad enough down here finding a job in the first place. Way I look at it, Tarantino, mad money he makes, he started in a video shop, and look at him now; he used to have his own section of 'cult' films, so I did the same, stuff like *Street Trash* and *Critters*, *Lost Boys*, *Kill Bill* (volumes one *and* two) and that, until the manager told me to take it down.

I got off the train and went to a pub near the station, just for a pint and a bit of Dutch courage before I went up there. There were some right rugby club hoorahs in black tie which is what you had to wear if you weren't going as a Hollywood film star. They were drinking champagne and making sure everyone knew it, particularly the locals who had to put up with students from the college all the time. One of the hoorahs kept looking over at me, then finally he comes over and says, 'Benny, isn't it?' I said no, John, and he goes, 'Look, everyone, Benny from *Crossroads*,' which is what they used to call me because of the way I talked. Anyway, they all roared with laughter and this bloke goes, 'Aren't you getting dressed up then?' and I said, 'I am dressed.' He said, 'Come over for some champagne,' which I knew meant 'Come over so we can take the piss out of you.' It was like that time at the freshers' disco when this girl, she was called Finola, pretended she wanted to slow-dance with me, I was dead nervous and she said, 'Don't worry, I won't bite,' and then she leads me off into a corner and starts undoing my belt and trousers and then all of a sudden some bloke comes up behind and pulls my trousers and pants down and they shone a bloody spotlight on my arse, everyone laughing, so I just pulled my trousers up and got out of there. So I said to him, 'No, I've got to be going,' and left it at that.

I had a little bit of a walk around the town, just killing time, it wasn't like I was all nostalgic or anything, in fact, I thought, why the hell had I come in the first place, what was the point? Waste of money. I'd just had this stupid idea that I would go. *I'll show you. I'll fucking show you. You won't show me, I'll show you.* Plus I got to wear the outfit and play a part, play the role, which I thought I was going to enjoy. It was just dark slacks, white T-shirt, blue denim shirt, brown jacket, white socks and black slip-ons. I started acting it out a bit, being mean and moody, and thought, *Will anyone guess?*

Finally I walked up the hill to the campus, and a black car drives past, honking its horn and it's the lot from earlier, all hanging out the window and making a racket, shouting 'BEN-EE, BEN-EE', so I flick a V and they throw a champagne bottle in the ditch and go roaring off.

I get there, and the place is as I remember it, it hasn't burned down, big main building with the quadrangle where the barbecue is, and I think, I never belonged here in the first place, I only came here because it was the only place I could get into, thickos like me and toffy-nosed posh-nobs who never did any work but went to college just to make it look good for their family. My folks were really pleased, they thought it was dead good I'd got into college even though it was a load of shit, but they weren't so pleased when I said I was jacking it in. I couldn't explain to them what it was like, my dad said it was a golden opportunity and that I was selfish. I don't really speak to him any more, I fell out with him about it. Once I got a job I moved out of home and got a bedsitter, it's OK, it's got its own sink and that. I can pay my own way now, the wages aren't brilliant from the video shop but it's enough, except that the manager keeps saying, 'Oh, we're probably going to have to close down, we're going to be put out of business by Blockbusters,' and I suggested why don't we do an 'adults-only section, horror and that, Blockbusters don't', and he says, 'People just get their pornos off the Internet now, it's not so embarrassing, so that won't work, no, we'll probably have to close down, best start looking for another job.' Yeah, doing what? I know what the old man would say, *if you had a degree* . . .

I sometimes see Mum, but not Dad, I couldn't explain to him the real reason I left college, how could I? I didn't really want to tell him what had happened, apart from the fact that I hated every minute of it and those bastards could make your life hell just for the sake of it, which they did, and it still gets to me sometimes and I think, *Christ, can't it just go away, why must I be reminded the whole time?* It's a pity, I used to get on with the old man when I was younger, we used to go to the beach and that when I was a kid, he was always going, 'I'm proud of you, son, you're going to be able to do what I never could' and all that sort of caper. Not any more, and instead I work in a poxy video shop where the manager doesn't even know the difference between *Night of the Living Dead* and *Return of the Living Dead*, he reckons 'Return' is a sequel but that's nothing to do with it. 'More brains, more brains,' the zombie goes in *Return*, that's what the manager needs, *more brains*! I reckon I could manage it better than him, easy, and not have to close down, but whenever I have an idea, like the blueys section or the cult corner, he goes, 'Just because you went to college you think you know better.'

I went in through the gates to the quadrangle. The person checking tickets said, 'It's black tie, or fancy dress.' I said, 'I'm *in* fancy dress'. She said, 'Who are you supposed to be?' I told her. She gave me a funny look, but let me in – I should think so after what I'd paid for the ticket and the train, nearly a week's bloody wages!

It was a bit much to take in at first, the big white tent, and all the people milling around dressed as Charlie Chaplin and Indiana Jones, Men in Black, all that sort of thing. There was jazz music playing and people having a drink up, and I could smell the burgers and thought, well, actually, I could quite enjoy this, might as well seeing as I've come all this way. I went and got a drink and a burger and sat down. Well, this girl comes up to me, and she's dressed as Catwoman. Not Catwoman from the film *Catwoman*, that was terrible, no, Catwoman from *Batman Returns*, played by Michelle Pfeiffer in the leather catsuit and mask. I thought the film sucked, I thought all the *Batman* films sucked, I never really liked the TV series either.

'Don't I know you?' she says. I was about to answer when she laughs and goes, 'Oh, of course, you're the boy that fancied Ronny!' and bursts out laughing. Ronny was my room-mate who put it about that I was a gay just to have a laugh at my expense, except he kept on about it, just to try and get me thrown out of halls so he could have the room to himself, complaining to the halls manager saying that I made him feel 'uncomfortable' when he came in from the shower; they made a big hoo-ha about it, so everyone believed it. But it sort of blew over because this girl Jenny that was on my course found out and she said we should pretend to be girlfriend and boyfriend to make them shut up so we did that for a while and sure enough they did shut up. But then they got me stoned one night, I don't know why I did it, I thought it was Ronny trying to make peace and get me involved with his mates so I went along with it, except it ended up with just me really stoned and I passed out. I was out my head and from what I heard they took a load of photos. I demanded off Ronny that he showed me but he just laughed and said they'll turn up on the Internet soon enough. I don't know if he ever did do that, and I couldn't stand people laughing and pointing and me not even knowing what the pictures were, it was really bloody shit from then on. *He wouldn't show me but I'll show him*.

This girl walks off, swinging her arse, and I thought, that is well out of order, I come all this way after all this time, I didn't even really want to come, and I get treated like that. I thought that after all these years they might at least say, 'Oh, it was only a joke, sorry about that, no harm intended,' maybe just be friendly. But no, it wasn't to be the case, and I thought, what if they *had* put them on the Net, what if people were looking at them to this day. It made me sick to my stomach to think they might be. I didn't dare do a search to see if they were, and anyway, what would I look for in the first place?

It had put me off my burger, so I tossed it into a flowerpot and drained the beer, then put the empty bottle into the inside of my jacket.

Catwoman was walking across the quadrangle to one of the doors that led inside the building. I followed her, sneaking through the door a bit after her, and quick enough to see the green door of the ladies' loo swinging closed. I waited a moment, then went in. No one else was in there, and one of the cubicle doors was shut, so I kicked it open and there she was sat on the toilet, and she screamed out, but I grabbed her by the throat, leaned forward and smashed the bottle on the cistern, then jammed the bottle in her face, then stepped out and shut the door. Then her friend walks in right behind me, it's Finola from the freshers' disco, she's dressed as *Bridget Jones's Diary* or something, I reckon she looks a bit fat compared to back then, and she goes, 'What the fuck are you doing you fucking pervert?' and I said, 'Don't worry, I won't bite,' and walk past her, then grab her by the face with both hands and force her mouth open, then clamp my teeth on her tongue and bite down hard and tear half her tongue off and spit it out, like in *Midnight Express*. There's blood all gushing out of her mouth so I push her away on to the floor so I don't get any blood on me and she bashes her head. I drag her into a cubicle, pull that cubicle door shut, then mop up the blood with some paper hand towels. After that I went back out to the party.

I'd had a few beers and it was starting to get dark, and people seemed to be enjoying themselves quite a lot. I started to relax a little and wander around, watched the jazz band for a bit, then there was a fire-eater, a magician, stuff like that, just getting my money's worth. Sure enough, it wasn't long before I saw Ronny, he was dressed as, well, I suppose it was meant to be Neo out of *The Matrix*, shades and long, gay leather jacket. The *Matrix* films were a right load of shit as well. Ronny must have thought he looked really cool but I thought he just looked like a bastard as usual. I was watching him when he sees me looking and says something to his mate (Olly? – dressed as *Reservoir Dogs*? He was a fucking bastard too) and then walks over.

'Fucking hell, if it isn't Benny from *Crossroads*! What have you come as, Benny? *Dumb and Dumber*?'

I gave him the finger, then turned and walked off, round the back of the marquee.

'Don't you fucking walk away from me!' he shouted out, and started after me. I'd ducked back into the shadows by the marquee and came out and got an arm around his neck, and snapped it, and he fell forward. Then Olly comes charging round and I'm ready for him, he runs right into the tent peg I'm holding out and it gets him in the throat, it makes a popping sound then a spurting noise, and he trips over Ronny. I rolled them both into the side of the marquee, out of sight. After that I thought, I now want to find those fuckers who were drinking champagne earlier! *And show them!*

They were stood in a group, swigging their drinks. They used to drink in the pub on the green, overlooking the cricket pitch. I went there once with some people from my course and of course we weren't supposed to go there really, they preferred us to go to The Beehive on the high street, so when we go in, one of their lot shouts out 'Give them a cider' and they all start singing 'I've got a brand new combine harvester' so we couldn't drink in peace. Anyway, one of the crowd had peeled off and was going for a slash in the shadows at the corner of the quadrangle. I followed him and stood behind him, giving him the eyeball, then I went and pulled his trousers right down round his ankles, he turned round, pissing everywhere and I whacked him in the jaw and he went over, still pissing. I stamped on his throat a few times until he was gurgling and left it at that. Then I thought it was time for a drink.

On my way to the bar I saw Jenny. She was quite nice, I'd liked her, always friendly, and she was dressed as Wonder Woman. She said, 'Hello, John, I didn't know you were coming, did you come all the way from Devon?' I said,

'Yes, I came on the train.' She said, 'John, who are you supposed to be?' I told her.

'Henry?' she said.

'Yes, *Henry: Portrait of a Serial Killer*. Directed by John McNaughton, 1986, not released until 1990.'

'I don't know it.'

'Henry was played by Michael Rooker. You might have seen him in *Cliffhanger*.'

'What's *Henry* about?' Jenny asked.

I started to answer and she went, 'John, I was joking, I think I know what it's about.' Then she said, 'Do you want a drink?' I nodded, and she went, 'I'm always happy to buy an old boyfriend a drink. Have you kept in touch with anyone else?' and I said no. Just then I heard a girl screaming outside in the quadrangle. I followed Jenny to the bar.

death row diary

dear marie

thanks for your letter. marie — is that french like paris, france? I did enjoy your letter. How comes you wrote to me? No, I cannot send emails marie, I was caught looking at ██████ on the internet and had my privileges revoked, so I will have to send a letter, and I know the warders sensor the letters the ████████████████.

You asked me what I did to be in here, I'd tell you Marie but then you might not write, let me just say none of it would have happened if my best buddy hadn't been ████████████ my wife and I wasn't handy with a Quarterlite .22 gauge hunting rifle. Hell, I was drinking heavy in those days, I admit it, it makes you not think straight.

Write back Marie, and could you send a photo?
Dabney, aka 'the scrote'

PS – my cellmate Chipmunk sure is jealous and says do you know any young boys who'd write him?

Marie –

Thanks for the picture. You look pretty, but could you send one showing your ██████ or ██████s? I would appreciate it. You asked if I had a picture, well know I don't but mebbe there'll be one in the papers when they send me to the chair!! If they send me – I might dies in jail before they juice me – my lawyer is trying to keep me out of the chair.

So these people that put you in touch with me Marie – do they pay you, Penetentiary Pen Pals? How does it work?

I do like your letter and sure would like to meet you, I know it is a long way to come for you. I don't have any visitors, say for example my best buddy and my wife, I killed them, oops (cold-blooded said the judge). And no family, I didn't kill them, that was natural causes except my daddy who got tore up by farm machinery.

You ask what I miss most – simple, ██████ , ██████ , ██████ , ██████ ! And beer.

Dabney
aka 'the scrote'

PS – you asked about my name, well, it's just a nickname I was given by the other fellas, I don't really know what it means

Hey marie —

I got your letter, but know photo. You said you'd sent a photo of your ████s, but I looked and looked and there was no photo. I no what happened, that ████████ Brenton took the photo, he checks the mail, he must have it the ████████ ████████ ██████. I will kill that ████, I'll tear off his ████████ ████and ████████ in his ████████. I'll ████ his dog and ████████ down his house.

Dabney

PS — thanks for the book on ~~recreation~~ reincarnation but can you send pictures out of magazines, J-Lo, britteny shit like that, oh yeah and Leonardo that's for my cellmate chipmunk, he likes fellas

Marie —

I haven't written you a while not because I forgot but because I couldn't. I been in the hole, they put me there after I attacked Brenton. He was on duty in the hall and I started giving the ████████ ████████████a bunch of ████████. I said to him, Brenton you ████████, you been ████████████to the photographs of Marie's ████s, don't deny it you pig-████████, and he comes at me with his stick. I wake up in the hole.

There's no letters from you but I guess they just taken them off me.

Dab

Well Marie

I ain't heard from you in two months. I guess they are still taking your letters, or that ████████ Brenton is taking them. I don't even know if you are even getting mine. My cellmate, chipmunk, he reckons there is more chance of him being made a cub scout than my letter getting through.

Well, in case it does, my reprieve fell on deaf ears, my lawyer said, he says 'let's go to Capitol Hill', but I said to him to hell with that, I sure am sick of rotting in a cage, might as well be done with it, I did what I did, I shot Joe in the spine and blasted that ████████████ Kathy in the ████████ face. Strap me in an throw the switch, do what you got to do.

Sure, I'll miss chipmunk and I'll miss your letters but sooner or later chipmunk'll get juiced for what he did to that boy and I don't get your letters anymore anyway.
Dab

Dear marie

I hope you get this letter. sorry I haven't written for so long. There ain't been much to write about until now. I'm getting turned crispy tomorrow, can you believe it? Finally it's happened and I thought I'd write one more time.

I'm allowed a final meal, I said, to hell with food, lemme have a beer-bust, they said no alcohol, I say shit it's hot where I'm goin, they said well have a coke.

I did send you a form for you to come and watch me go,

but I ain't heard from you. I guess it is a long way.

For the meantime I am in my own cell. I sure do miss chipmunk and the stories he told me about what he did to that boy down in the Carrybeyan before he got caught. Hell he could talk all night ████ about the kids ████ off and I wouldn't mind.

Well marie, if you don't hear from me again say a prayer for me but make it awful loud else satan won't hear, heh heh.

Dab

aka The Scrote

Dear Marie

We fried that fucker today, that sick individual! He was crying when we took him down there – fucking lowlife! It makes me puke to see them acting all sorrowful after what he did. I guess I can only be thankful that it was because of him I got to meet you.

Those last photographs you sent me were awesome. How the hell did you get your ankles round the back of your head like that?

I'm due leave in a few weeks, I plan to fly out to South C and fuck your brains out (sure I'll bring my billy club!).

Send more photos you dirty whore! (ps – no, I ain't showing them round the other boys, what do you think I am, an animal?!)

Brenton

the expedition

We had to eat the last of the huskies today. Tuffers was distraught. He loved those dogs. I wasn't best happy either; it was all skin and bones, the meat very stringy. Tuffers pleaded with me, he said, can't we eat the flapjacks instead? I said Tuffers, you know as well as I, those flapjacks are for emergencies, for when we're in a spot. He said, isn't this a spot? and I said, Tuffers, a spot is when you're really up against it, like the time in 1908 when three of us travelled eight miles on an ice floe no more than four metres square. I'm getting Jenkins to make me some lovely warm mittens from the husky pelt and maybe a hat.

Poor old Tonkinson. First he suffered the indignity of losing all his fingers and toes to frostbite — now most all his feet have gone as well. He totters along on two stumps —

God bless him, there's nothing to attach the snowshoes to. I've heard murmurings among the men that maybe Tonks, not me, should be the one being pulled along on the sledge. I addressed it when we made camp – I said it was complete rot and nonsense! If Tonks was to lay prone and be dragged, his muscles would clean waste away and then what good would he be to the expedition? We might just as well toss his body down the crevasse that Jones fell down yesterday. (I can't help but chuckle when I see Tonks try to sip a hot beverage – bereft of digits with which to manipulate the tin handle, he has to grasp the hot metal with both stumps – he does cry out, the poor chap!)

Back in the mother country, people say to me, they say, Shepperton, why do you do it? Why on earth do you put yourself and your men through it every time? What reason, what purpose? – Good God, man, there's a war raging, and you insist on embarking on an expedition, and for why? For why? And I reply thus: did one caveman watch the other rubbing two sticks together and ask 'For why?' What discoveries, what wonders might we find? Professor Gatehouse has unearthed two very rare lichen already! But do I turn back merely on account of the extraordinary dangers? I do not. Onwards.

We lost six men in an avalanche this afternoon. We tried, and tried again, to dig them out, but to no avail. We dug, and dug, but by the time we unearthed Tonks's stumps protruding from the ice, it was clear they were all lost. A terrible tragedy, a tragic waste of good, irreplaceable men. Worst of all, we lost the Sherpa chef. I shall miss his cheese flans. Jenkins has hinted that the avalanche might have been triggered by my calling out with the loudhailer. I was only seeing if there were any Himalayan mountain men who might have some goat meat to trade – for the men. I always put my men first. I shall severely reprimand Jenkins for that. Not verbally mind. No flapjacks for *him*.

It is so cold now, so cold . . . I can barely hold a pen to write this. I'm dictating it instead, to Tuffers – it gives him something to do, takes his mind off our killing and eating the dogs. How he loved those huskies, gambolling with them in the snow, nuzzling their warm, wet noses; they even slept alongside him by the fireside. They were like children to him, really they were. Oh dear, that does seem to have set Tuffers off. I will resume the journal when Tuffers has regained his composure.

Things are not looking good. We are down to four men. Myself, Jenkins, Tuffers and Oakes. Gatehouse plunged to his doom trying to pluck a curious-looking plant from a ledge on the ascent. He slipped and was dangling there, crying out – I had to cut him loose, lest he pull the rest of us down with him. Jenkins pointed out later that Gatehouse wasn't actually roped to anyone else. Details! I said to him. I'm a man of action! I did what I considered right at the time. That quietened him down.

Oakes made a brave if foolhardy gesture last night. The four of us were huddled in the tent, warming ourselves on the pathetic flames from a demolished wooden snowshoe. It had become apparent there were only flapjacks enough for three. Oakes, who had been drinking a good deal of hot tea, claimed he needed to go outside to relieve himself. 'I won't be a minute,' he said, as he lifted the tent flap and disappeared into the howling wind and the black swirling night. I instructed Jenkins to close the tent flap securely, saying, 'It's bloody freezing in here.' Not a little later, sat expecting Oakes to return, a most eerie thing occurred. The wind, wailing and seemingly crying out, buffeted the tent flap as if it was being battered by a human hand. The mind can play strange tricks on a man up here in the thin air of the frozen heights. But still no sign of Oakes. He was never to return. I realise now he was sacrificing himself for the team.

Just me now. I sent Jenkins and Tuffers out to reconnoitre to find Oakes. They, too, did not return. I could only think the worst, and fortified myself with the rest of the flapjacks. I shall make it to the summit, I shall! I will carry on for the men. It's what they would have wanted.

What luck. I met some Norwegians at the top. They had plenty of supplies so I had a good nosh-up.

There was, unfortunately, a bit of a set-to – they claim the Norwegian flag was planted first, but I insisted we got there at roughly the same time – besides, we lost our flag in the avalanche. Next time I'll pack a reserve. I'm convinced I've got frostbite and have persuaded Jurgens to let me lie on one of the sledges on the way down.

Last night, one of the Norwegians caught me trying to pull down their flag. Most embarrassing, and Jurgens tells me I'll have to walk down now.

A hero's welcome in London – a telegram from the King – an offer (rather lucrative!) to serialise my adventures in the *Piccadilly Gazette* – and a banquet in my honour at the Cesil Hotel. I was asked, where next? I replied, somewhere unexplained, treacherous and just plain beastly. Will advertise for men in the morning.

G. J. Shepperton, Euston, 1917

happy days

Hammond steered the car along the gravel driveway and stopped in front of the house. Malloy hasn't done too badly for himself at all, Hammond thought, pulling on the handbrake. Little wonder, though. As he got out of the car the front door of the house opened. There was Malloy – older, greyer, but smiling still.

'All right if I leave her here?'

'Perfect, wonderful, come in, come in.'

Hammond lifted his overnight case off the passenger seat.

'No need locking it, no one around here to steal it!' Malloy said.

Hammond was an old school friend of Joseph Malloy, the noted, award-winning research chemist. Malloy, among other things, had invented and patented a

49

super-preservative, which had proved so effective and long-lasting it was now being used by most of the big food manufacturers. Hence the impressive pile. He had invited Hammond up for the weekend. They hadn't seen each other for years. The years intervene, but meeting an old school friend is like turning back the clock – in a moment, those years dissolve. Professional reputations and personal ambitions to be checked at the door. Old jokes resurface, youth takes over once more. You could be a distinguished research chemist, or a partner in a law firm – high achievers if you like, as these two were; Birtles School seemed to mass-produce them – but it was all reduced to japery and fond memories in the warm glow of an all too rare reunion.

Malloy patted Hammond firmly on the back. 'Good to see you, Peter, so awfully good to see you, do go through.' He gestured into the hall. 'I'll show you your room directly, but how about a drink? You've had a bit of a drive.'

'Why not?' Hammond said, following Malloy through a door into the lounge. Malloy made his way over to a table stocked with decanters.

'You find it OK?'

'No problem.'

'Sorry to be so covert. You see, no one knows where I am. Not my sponsors, not the committees, not anyone. Gone to ground if you like. Quite necessary with what I'm working on at the moment. You'd be surprised at the interruptions one gets. I decided some time ago, no disturbance, none. Apart from welcome ones such as yourself.'

'I understand. I feel quite privileged to be the guest of such an eminent scientist.'

'Nonsense, nonsense, friends together, that's all.'

Hammmond surveyed the room. It was rather plush and well appointed – not to mention neat and tidy. 'This is a change from your study at Birtles,' Hammond said. 'That used to resemble an explosion in a test-tube factory.'

Malloy chuckled. 'Yes, yes. I couldn't manage this on my own. I have someone who does for me.'

'A maid?'

'Does a bit of everything,' Malloy said, turning and proffering a glass. 'Scotch OK? – I put some ice in it.'

'Perfect,' Hammond said. He noticed Malloy's cheeks were flushed, his eyes all atwinkle, and wondered if he hadn't already had a few stiffeners himself. He took a sip of the drink.

'Yes, the old girl is cooking for us tonight. She's fairly handy all round.'

Hammond raised an eyebrow. 'This wouldn't happen to be your wife you're talking about?'

Malloy had propped himself by the mantelpiece over the fireplace. 'God, no, no time for that. Hired help, that's all.'

'Still too busy with the old test tubes.'

'Indeed.'

'You don't work here, surely?'

'I have a lab — a converted prefab — in the grounds round the back.'

'I should like to see it.'

'Not much to see. Just like my room at Birtles, only bigger! And you? Did you find time for a family?'

'Divorced. Two kids, off at school themselves now.'

'Really?' Malloy's gaze moved off towards a silver-framed picture in the middle of the mantelpiece. 'School, eh?'

'Well, I never did,' Hammond said, moving forward to look at the picture. 'I haven't seen that in an age!' He reached to pick it up. 'Don't mind if I — ?'

'Do, do, by all means!' Malloy said.

Hammond rested his drink on the mantel and held the picture in both hands. It was the five of them — himself, Paiser, Marlow, Turner, with Malloy standing behind them in the background — the 'Roaring Boys' — sat round the table in the common room at Birtles, in (literally) high spirits, toting ridiculous cigars, raising a toast — Hammond grasping a bottle of absinthe, glasses and ashtrays in front of them — a moment of glory captured in that one picture, celebrating their last day at Birtles before they set out into the world, and to hell with the rules! The gang broken up finally, off their separate ways to university and careers and LIFE. They were good, sturdy, intelligent lads. But life holds in store a good supply of surprises however good, sturdy and intelligent you are, Hammond had found that out, and, no doubt, the rest of them had too.

'How long ago?' Hammond mused.

'Thirty years or so.'

'My God. I never did get a copy of this picture. I wonder if –'

'You could get a copy? Of course, of course. Happy days, eh?'

'Yes – happy days.' Hammond scrutinised the photograph. He gazed, quite understandably, at himself, looking at the camera, fighting drunk and full of vim. Brave in the face of the impending years. Would he have been so brave had he known what they would bring, for him, for all of them?

'Do you – have you kept in touch with any of the others?' Malloy asked.

'Our paths have crossed occasionally. But – over the years . . .'

'I know, I know, I have tried – I tried – to get us all together . . . hellish thing to do.'

'I remember – the Roaring Boys reunion.'

'No one could ever spare the same weekend.' Malloy shook his head. 'I never gave up though. I had to settle for visits from you all on separate occasions.'

'I didn't think of you as much of a one for nostalgia. Too busy trying to stumble across your own penicillin.'

'Oh, you know. I have my work, and sometimes it feels like nothing but. But these days – well – I don't have much beyond that.' Malloy took a good swallow of his Scotch.

'So you've seen the others?' Hammond asked.

'Yes, well, tried to keep track, you know, the odd letter, the odd visit. Difficult to stay in touch.'

'It's a shame really,' Hammond said, carefully replacing the picture. 'So that's what I owe this invitation to? Sort of a partial reunion.'

'Exactly, exactly. Wonderful to see you. Now – I'll show you to your room – maybe you'd like to get freshened up – we can have another drink – then supper a little later. Oh, I nearly forgot.' Malloy reached into his pocket and pulled out a tie. He handed it to Hammond.

Hammond unfolded it and held it up.

'The old school tie,' Malloy said.

'So I see.'

Malloy slid his thumb under the school tie he was already wearing.

'I presume this is de rigueur dinner-dress,' Hammond said.

'Indeed,' Malloy said. 'Now I'll show you to your room.'

Malloy was reclining in a deep armchair, drinking another Scotch, when Hammond came back down, wearing his tie.

'Help yourself to a drink, old chap,' he said.

Hammond went over to the table with the decanters.

'Ice in the round thing,' Malloy told him.

'Did you hear about Paiser?' Hammond asked, pouring himself a drink.

'Hear what?'

'About his disappearance.'

'Disappearance?'

'It was only a couple of inches buried in the middle of the paper. I only happened to read it because it said "Diplomat Missing". I think it's just a scare – he might have gone to ground like yourself.'

'What's the line on it?'

'Nothing really. He went away on business midweek a few weeks ago and hasn't been seen since.'

'Really. Old Paiser. He always was a bit of a gadabout.'

'Which is why the diplomatic service suited him, I suppose. I should think he'll turn up. Probably in some godforsaken colony where the phone lines are down.'

'I didn't know we had any colonies left. Do sit down, old boy.'

Hammond made himself comfortable in a chair opposite Malloy. 'So, what is it you're working on at the moment?' Hammond said.

'You as well, eh? You'll get nothing out of me, old chum!'

'More food stuff?'

'Oh no. Not that.' Malloy chuckled to himself, his eyes glinting as he looked into his glass. 'Something quite different. But along those lines . . . No seriously, nothing too exciting. Or rather, nothing worth talking about. If you ask me to explain it, you'll wish you hadn't.'

'You either *get* science, or you don't, I've always thought. And I never did.'

'Well then, let's not discuss it. Let's talk about something else. Here,' Malloy said, raising his glass. 'To the Roaring Boys.'

'To the Roaring Boys,' Hammond said. They chinked glasses.

'Ah – wearing the tie. Good, good.'

And with that, they settled in to an afternoon of reminiscing.

The Roaring Boys – so named, as Hammond remembered it, from an Oliver Goldsmith play – a group of reckless gadabouts, aficionados of William Blake and his 'road of excess', aesthetes, roustabouts who exuded youthful bluster, drank feverishly and generally got up to no good. The five of them were all in the same house – and their modus operandi was not just to upset the apple cart, but to tip it clean over and stamp the fruit to a pulp. At weekends they would go to the local country pubs, forbidden, and get into fights with the riff-raff. During the week, one or another would find himself in front of the housemaster or, better still, the head. When Turner had been expelled for scaling the walls of one of the girls' boarding houses and breaking into the dormitory at night, the remaining Roaring Boys spelled out in weedkiller a crude insult on the lawn in front of the headmaster's house. In the right light, it could still be read weeks afterwards and the whole lawn had to be returfed. The Roaring Boys had smuggled Turner back into school, drunk the twice-weekly drinking club dry and locked him in the cupboard for the night, where he was found the following morning by the cleaner, bolt upright and surrounded by broken bottles. Their pièce de résistance had been hanging an effigy of the headmaster from the gym roof on speech day, the crude dummy with its huge nose and bald head sparing the parents and staff no blushes before it was cut down by the gym teacher. Before that, Malloy had concocted a solution that they poured into the swimming pool the night before swimming day – which in the morning had turned the pool bright red underneath a two-foot layer of yellow foam. With each member of the gang bringing his own peculiar skill to bear, all manner of capers were played out by these thoroughly bright, easily bored renegades.

After several drinks, Hammond asked Malloy to show him round the grounds. He wanted to try, if he could, to coax the conversation away, for a moment at least, from the glory days of the Roaring Boys; it seemed to be making

Malloy very sentimental, verging on tearful. Much more whisky and fond recollection might see the man weeping. Hammond remembered Malloy was a sensitive sort – despite his pragmatic mind and eccentric manner – and he, more than any of them, seemed to value the kinship they enjoyed at school dearly, and was clearly the most upset at their disbanding. He had never said as much, but it was in his eyes when they shook hands farewell all those years ago, for the last time.

'That's the lab,' Malloy said, waving towards a moss-green-coloured corrugated-iron prefab, set back down some stone steps and overhung by branches from the woods beyond. 'Nothing to see there,' Malloy continued as Hammond went down the steps and peered in through a dusty window. Beside this was a padlocked door. Inside, he made out what he thought was on old gym vaulting horse, surrounded by clutter. 'I say, isn't that – ?' 'Really, nothing to see,' Malloy said, not moving from his place at the top of the steps. Hammond peered in again briefly, then walked back up the steps.

After a cursory stroll around the garden, they stood on the back lawn and looked out over the woods at the edge of the grounds. 'If only we could have stayed together,' Malloy said. 'Silly, isn't it? Hanging on like that.'

'Not at all,' Hammond said, patting his friend on the shoulder.

'The Roaring Boys,' Malloy said, wistfully. 'We blazed for a moment, didn't we?'

'We did that.'

'Just for a moment,' Malloy said, narrowing his eyes, his hands thrust deep in his pockets. 'Well – let's go back to the house.'

Supper was served in a rather austere dining room. The dark wood panelling, and shelves bare aside from the odd leather-bound book, added to the gloom. It reminded Hammond of nothing less than the dank hall where they'd eaten as schoolboys. It seemed empty with just the two of them, and only the maid for company when she brought in the dishes.

'Pity we couldn't have got all the boys together at once, eh?' Malloy said. He seemed to have become quite morose as the afternoon had worn on and the drinks had taken hold.

'Even if we could have,' Hammond countered, 'we'd have been one down.'

'What do you mean?' Malloy asked, pausing with his fork halfway to his mouth.

'What with old Paiser disappearing.'

'Ah yes. But like you say, I'm sure he'll show up.'

They ate in silence for a while.

'So, you never thought of a wife – any dalliances, anything like that?'

'Not really, no. I suppose it never really crossed my mind.'

'Do you not get a bit lonely out here all alone?'

'As long as I'm busy it's fine,' Malloy said.

Hammond didn't think he could do that. However busy he was with work, he'd relied on his wife to be there when he came home. He was totally devastated when she'd left. Apparently *he'd* been spending too much time at work. Maybe Malloy had the right idea – after all, what sort of a life was it being a wife to someone who was never there? He imagined – knowing Malloy as he did – it would be no life at all. Malloy had been known to disappear into his 'lab' for days on end and not see daylight, emerge quite fatigued and bedraggled but sated. By the sounds of it, that hadn't changed. A scientist did not become esteemed and sought-after without bloody hard work and no doubt all-consuming endeavour. Hence a maid and a lab *in situ*. He had reaped the rewards – the secluded house, the ornate grounds, all of it probably lost on Malloy, who no doubt would have been content with a fold-out bed next to his workbench.

'Why the big house – all this paraphernalia?' Hammond said. 'If you don't mind me asking?'

'Not at all. When I won the prize – it was a lot of money you know – not to mention the dividends for the patent – ridiculous.'

'I read about that.'

'Well – it was on a whim really – and I wanted some-where – how shall I put it? – off the beaten track, as I mentioned earlier. Partly that – partly, I thought, it might make a good retreat. Perhaps I've become philosophical in my old age –'

'Hardly old.'

'Hardly young either, eh? But, I thought, maybe it wasn't much of a life. Beavering away all the time in my lab . . . it's why I tried to organise the reunion. Does that sound silly?'

'Of course not. Maybe at a stretch we could still organise it. It would be a wonderful location. Make a weekend of it.'

'Exactly what I thought. And like you say, all hope is not lost. Not at all.'

'If Paiser shows up.'

'Hmm. Yes. Indeed.' Malloy reached and poured himself another glass of wine. 'You?'

'Yes, thanks.'

'You know when it gets me?' Malloy said, pouring the wine. Hammond shook his head. 'On a Sunday night. As it is getting dark. I think of how we'd all retreat to our studies after supper, to catch up on all the work we'd neglected during the week. Get it done quickfast, then decamp for a cigarette on the fire escape before lights out, and then . . . the Monday-morning blues. I think of that on a Sunday – where we all are now – some sat with their families, some away on business – me, I'm usually tinkering away! Trying to take my mind off it. I just can't stand Sunday nights.' He stopped and stared at the ceiling for a moment, then snapped out of it. 'Enough! Tomorrow's tomorrow. I have a treat for us later. With the cigars,' Malloy said, grinning.

'This is quite a treat already. Good to see you,' Hammond said, raising his glass.

They chinked glasses once more.

'Thanks for coming, Hammond, many thanks for coming.' Malloy had reached across the table and grasped Hammond's forearm quite tightly. Malloy's moroseness seemed to have gripped *him* even tighter.

'No problem at all,' Hammond said.

'Was for me,' Malloy said. 'Tracking you down. Tracking anyone down. Sent on a wild-goose chase.'

'Imagine if one of us had wanted to track *you* down.'

Malloy frowned. 'If they'd wanted to . . .' he said, his voice trailing off. 'The reason I asked you here,' Malloy went on. 'All this work – I mean – it's all very well – accolades, prizes, pats on the back – the house – the achievement, if you will, people wanting to know what you're doing, following your every move. But, looking back, the only time there was real fire – real – *passion* – was back then, you know. I've come to see that now. The Roaring Boys. What a team, eh? What a team. I valued that. I value that over this, over anything really. Daft thing is, you don't realise it at the time. You don't grasp it. You can't. I suppose that's what science is about – trying to grasp the universe and make sense of it. Grasp a second and hold it and look at it – dissect the molecules – that's all it is. Life just passes by and we try to understand and explain it – for what? The greater good, the next generation. I don't know, I really don't. There's no making sense of it. The molecules all crumble in the end. I mean, what is there, after youth, really, after your youth drags on and peters out, what is there, except memories, memories and drudgery? Is that what we become – drudges? *Sic transit gloria mundi!*'

Malloy was staring at Hammond as if he expected a response. Hammond shrugged weakly, uneasily. 'I suppose it does.'

'But the Roaring Boys! You see, in my mind, I'm still there. I'm still there.'

'They always said schooldays were the best days of your life.'

'They did, yes, they said that, exactly, they told us that much. I never believed it – no one ever does. How could they be? we asked, how could they possibly be? But it's true. It's absolutely true. It gets truer with every year. Money, success, all that . . . you can keep that. Keep it all. Schooldays.'

'Maybe you should become a teacher.'

'I thought of that, I did. But wouldn't that just make it worse? I would end up preaching to them – enjoy your schooldays? No, I couldn't do that. I couldn't do that at all.'

The maid cleared the last of the plates. 'How about this treat?' Hammond asked, trying to lift Malloy's ebbing spirits.

It certainly did the trick – Malloy snapped out of his reverie. 'Indeed, yes,' he said, pushing back his chair and throwing down his napkin. He went over and unlocked a cabinet. 'You'll remember this.' He withdrew a green bottle from the cabinet. Only it wasn't the bottle that was green, but the contents.

Hammond was momentarily alarmed. 'Oh no.'

'Oh yes,' Malloy grinned.

It was absinthe. The same dangerous stuff as they'd been drinking all those years ago – Turner had brought several bottles of the stuff back from Spain for that very occasion, their last day. From what Hammond could recall, once the absinthe did its work – an effect unlike any other form of alcohol – they'd become quite demented. Hammond was not sure he wanted to revisit it now, and the repercussions – not so much a hangover, as a horror show. But he would have to defer to his host, who was eagerly unscrewing the cap. Malloy poured two large glasses, and set them down on the table. 'Have a go on that, old boy. Get it down you. I'll get the cigars.' Malloy plonked the bottle down in front of Hammond and went back to the cabinet.

Hammond sniffed at the green liquid, then tentatively took a sip. He neither remembered the taste, nor relished it. He picked up the bottle to examine the label, except that there was no label. Nor was this absinthe. Hammond felt his body begin to stiffen, quite horribly. It was not how he remembered the effects of the drink, if he could have recalled them at all, but it had not been like this, the sudden hardening sensation in the veins that he felt, his limbs losing all feeling, his lips and face growing cold. He wanted to call out, for something was wrong, but his jaw was frozen rigid.

Malloy tilted Hammond's chair and dragged it back through a set of double doors into an adjacent room, a room he liked to call the 'common room'. It was painted light green, with a Birtles' school banner tacked to the wall. They were all there, gathered round the table – Paiser, Marlow, Turner, all wearing their ties and rictus grins of celebration. And now Hammond, manoeuvred into his position among the group, clutching the bottle of absinthe. Half-filled ashtrays and glasses littered the table. Malloy stood in front of the tableau and smiled. He returned to the dining room and took a long gulp of his drink, then went back through.

He checked through the viewfinder of the camera on a tripod in front of the table, and, seeing it was correctly positioned, set the timer, then moved round to the back of the group and assumed his pose, and waited for the shutter to go off. Happy days, he thought to himself, feeling his body stiffen.

dogging

Jon was well up for doing a bit of 'dogging' – he'd read about it in the paper then he borrowed a dogging video off Tony, and that decided him even more. Jon explained to me that dogging is when a load of blokes gather at a motorway lay-by and then there's this woman in a car and she does the lot of them, in the back of the car, on the bonnet, even through the bloody window, he reckoned. No one knows anyone, it's all anonymous, 'no names, no pack drill', Jon had said.

Well, Jon signed up on a dogging website, fiver a month it was, and they tell you the 'dogging spots' up and down the country where you'd definitely find a car with a right slag in the back seat ready for it. These women, Jon told me, you didn't even have to pay them, and they were well up for a bit of dirty behaviour, and Jon reckoned he was just the man to dole it out. 'What about your missus?' I asked him, and he winks and goes, 'What that old trout doesn't know will not hurt her!'

Anyway, Jon found a dogging spot off of the website which was quite nearby, off the M11, and three of us went along, me, Jon and Terry. I was map-reading and also going to video the event on my camcorder for Jon. Everyone was dead quiet on the way up, in anticipation I suppose, until Terry pipes up, 'What if she's a proper boiler, Jon?' and Jon goes, 'You've seen the video, they were proper tasty, and up for it.' Then Terry goes, 'Yeah, but that was a video,' and Jon goes, 'I'll drop you at Little Chef if you want, Tel,' and Terry shuts up after that.

I told Jon to turn off because I thought it was our exit but it turns out to be the slip road off towards Ockley, so we have to drive all the way along to the roundabout and come back to get on the motorway, and Jon goes, 'You proper doughnut, there'll be a queue by the time we get there,' and Terry slaps me on the back of the head.

We finally find the place and sure enough there's this car waiting, an old blue Austin Allegro parked right over the other side of the car park, near the slope to the exit lane back to the motorway. I say, 'What are they parked all the way over there for?' and Terry goes, 'In case they need to make a quick getaway, you plum.' I go, 'Is it illegal?' and Terry goes, 'No, dogscock, the coppers love people having sex on the bonnet of their cars in broad daylight.' I say,

'What, even if there's families around?' and he replies, 'Just shut the fuck up.'

Well, we get out of the car and creep over there, and I start up the video camera. This bloke comes over, he's wearing a T-shirt and jeans, tats and that on his arm, he says, 'You boys want to do some dogging?' and Jon goes, 'All right if we tape it?' pointing to me, and the bloke goes, 'Do what you fucking like.' We go over to the car and the boys start peering in the back window, Jon going, 'Gorr, look at that, she's got nice big ones, take that off, love, oh yes, 'ave some of that. Oh that's lovely, oh yes, spread them, what did I tell you, Terry, what did I say?' and Terry goes, 'Yeah, do what he says, love!' Finally the bloke with the tats says, 'Are you lads going to do anything or just stand there all day? She wants to be home in time for *Corrie*.' So Terry drops his trousers, and goes to me, 'Don't film me arse, film her,' and then goes, 'Wind down the window, love, I've got something for you!' and Jon's gone round the other side by this point and got in the back door with the woman. All of a sudden Terry's going, 'Ooh yeah,' and thrusting forward through the window. I film over Terry's shoulder to watch Jon-boy getting stuck in inside. The woman's got blonde frizzy hair (peroxide), stockings and suzzies, nothing else, and Jon is clambering on top of her. The bloke with the tats is standing behind me, jerking away there, watching. I decide it's time for a bit of dogging myself, so I open up the front door of the car and climb in, first of all filming Jon going full steam ahead from behind, while she's giving Terry a seeing-to through the window, then, still holding the camera, I undo my trousers and try to get in position so she can give it a right sucking (she looks the type), but I can't manage it because my head is pushed up against the roof of the car – not much room in these things. So I think the best thing is to put my legs through first, and I do that but they get stuck in between the front seats, so I can't move and end up filming the ceiling. I tried to get up but can't and Jon goes, 'Watch your feet.' I was jammed right in there, wriggling around trying to sit up, then all of a sudden there's this jolt and the car starts rolling, I've only gone and let off the handbrake by accident, it was sticking right up my arse and I must have pushed it down; Jon doesn't notice at first, but Terry does, his balls are hanging through the window and the bird's got a hold of his nodger, so he has to sidestep, going, 'What the bloody hell's going on?' then the car picks up speed and he has to leap up and grab the roof rack and hang on for dear life, he's shouting out and then the bird lets go and Terry falls off and there's an almighty thud like the back wheel has gone over his head. I try to see what's happened but all I can see is the bloke with tats in the background standing there pulling his plonker. Jon goes, 'What the fuck have you done, put the brake on!' and I tell him I can't move, so he goes, 'Steer left, steer left,' and I say, 'My left or your left?' and he goes, 'What the hell are you talking about,

STEER LEFT!' So I reach behind me and grab the steering wheel and I must have done it the wrong way because the car whistles down the exit ramp towards the motorway, it's all gone silent apart from the noise of the wheels drumming on the road, and then the road flattens out and there's a horn going off behind us and a screech then something goes crash, right into us, and the car spins round then something else hits us and the car flips over into the ditch.

When I come to all I can hear is Jon going, 'Me bollocks, me bollocks,' then I hear someone outside going, 'Look at the state of this.' Then a fireman sticks his head through the broken window and says to the woman, whose eyes are shut and is bleeding from the nose, 'What's your name, love? Just tell us your name,' and Jon mumbles, 'No names, no pack drill,' then passes out, and the fireman looks over his shoulder and says, 'Go get the saw.'

Well, we get in the papers, front page of the *Argus*, photos, the lot, I lost my job on account of it, Jon was none too happy about it because his missus found out (course she did, they have it delivered); worse than that, the tape I took's doing the rounds. The police confiscated it when they got there. I reckon someone down the cop shop is knocking out copies, what else could it be? Jon's wife is threatening to leave him for making her the laughing stock around town, and there's going to be a court case, something to do with indecent behaviour and reckless driving, so Jon will probably lose his job on the white vans. Terry is on crutches and the woman is still in hospital, severe concussion and whatnot. The bloke with the tats just disappeared apparently but they reckon the woman will tell them who he is when she comes to. Jon reckons it's all my fault and says he's going to kill me when he sees me but he's always saying things like that, and anyway it was his idea, and if anything it's really the fault of that bloke for having a car with a dodgy handbrake. Anyway, I reckon it'll all blow over in time and we'll be able to have a laugh about it down the pub soon enough, but I haven't been down there just yet, I heard they're playing the tape on the big screen when the footy's not on, bastards. One thing's for sure, I ain't bloody going dogging again in a hurry.

to hell with hollywood

No sooner had Finlayson stepped off the Greyhound than he was accosted by someone he would later describe as a 'ne'er-do-well, a street urchin with a bandanna wrapped around his head.'

Finlayson stood on the sidewalk, mopping his brow with his breast-pocket handkerchief, commenting to himself that it was a relief to be off that dreadful bus, out in the cool air of early-evening, downtown Los Angeles . . . when the little man ran up to him.

'Give it up, buddy,' the little man said, laying a hand on Finlayson's sole piece of luggage, a brown leather briefcase with two snap-locks and embossed with his initials.

'DESIST!' Finlayson cried out.

The impertinent little man bared his teeth and tugged at the case. 'Cough it up!'

73

At which point Finlayson grabbed him by the scruff of his neck, and pulled him up on tiptoes. 'Everyone in town wants what's in this bag,' he said. 'Do you really think I'm going to give it to the first person who asks?'

By now, the dirty little bastard that Finlayson was holding off the ground looked confused. Finlayson let him drop.

'What's in the bag?' the man asked, rubbing his neck.

'Something very valuable. Something that's going to make me RICH. Available only to the highest bidder . . .' He held the briefcase aloft.

'You're crazy in the head, buddy,' the man said. 'You've got nothing in there.'

Finlayson started to speak. 'No one's interested,' the little man said, and walked away.

Checking into the Bel Air Motel, not to be confused with the Bel Air Hotel, where celebrities stay around Oscar time, the manager looked at Finlayson's registration card.

'What's this you've written here?'

'That's my address in London.'

'Don't try to impress me. I'm not easily impressed. I get people staying here from all over the world – I get Indians, Japanese, I even get visitors from England.'

'London, England.'

'Don't get smart with me. All I'm saying is I need an address inside the USA, for *this* registration to be valid.'

'I'm not –'

'Either you have a domestic address – or you don't.'

'I can give you a New York address.'

'Write it down. Flew in from New York today, huh? I thought I could smell something funny.'

'Actually I came on the Greyhound bus.'

'Jesus Christ. The bus is strictly for bums. You coulda flown cheaper.'

'Oh no. I wanted to see the country – the people.'

'Meet some nice people, did you, on the bus?'

'Actually I didn't speak to anyone at all.'

'People don't like to have their personal space interrupted.'

'Invaded.'

'What?'

'Invaded. Not interrupted.'

'Don't interrupt me. Like I was saying – people like to keep themselves to themselves.'

The manager picked up the registration card and looked at it. 'Three addresses. One in England. One in New York. And now one in Los Angeles. Isn't that something. Should I get the bellhop to take your luggage to your room, your majesty?'

'There's no need. I only have this.' Finlayson took his case and key and went to find his room.

Finlayson had decided to come to Hollywood on a whim, and to take the town by storm, which was, in his opinion, the best way to take it. He wasn't like these other schmuckleheads trying to break into the movies, touting their wares. What he had, no one else could even dream of. He felt he had it made. Knowing what he knew, how could he feel otherwise?

He lay back on the bed, flicking through the channels with the remote control. He flicked backwards and forwards, watching bits and pieces of each programme. Drivel, he thought to himself. Repetitive drivel. The universal language, the world over. He turned off the TV and decided to get some sleep.

Finlayson stayed in bed until late, dozing on and off, until he felt fully rested. When he finally woke up he wondered what the hell he was doing there, and then he remembered and became calm. He walked to the nearest restaurant for lunch.

He took a seat in a booth on his own, and ordered a hamburger and a cup of coffee.

He signalled the waitress over to his table when he'd finished.

'You want more coffee?' she asked. She started to pour him some coffee.

'I wondered if you had a toothpick. It's just – I've got something stuck –'

'In your teeth, I bet. Hey, Hank,' she called back behind her. 'We got any toothpicks?'

'Toothpicks? Christ! For who?' The voice came from in the kitchen. 'Is it for the guy that speaks weird?'

The waitress blushed. 'Sorry about that.'

'It's no bother,' Finlayson told her.

'So, have we got any?' No answer. There was a hiss of steam and a shriek. 'I'll go look,' the waitress said. A customer from another table was trying to get her attention. But she walked past and ignored him. Finlayson sat there uncomfortably while she was gone.

A little while later she came back and handed him several dozen toothpicks in a plastic container. 'I didn't even know we had these.'

Finlayson shook one loose. 'It's very good of you, thank you.'

'You're polite!' she laughed. 'It's me that's supposed to be polite. I'm going to have to give you a tip.'

'Why, thank you.'

She laughed again. The other customer called out, 'Hey, *miss*!' She ignored him. 'Where are you from? Is it France?'

Finlayson, agitated that he was holding up the other diners, told her, 'Yes, Paris actually.'

She clapped her hands together. 'That's five bucks you owe me, Hank,' she called back. A moan came from the kitchen. Then Hank emerged. His face was all red and puffy. He had a towel against one eye.

'Quit gabbin,' will ya? I just nearly half burned myself to death and all you are doin' out here is gabbin'. Will you please serve the goddam customers?'

The waitress went off again.

She sneaked back again when Hank went back into the kitchen. Finlayson was working a toothpick around in his mouth.

'What are you doing in LA?'

He tapped his briefcase. 'I've come to sell this.'

'You came to LA to sell a valise?'

'No – what's in it.'

'What *is* in it?'

'A film script.'

'Oh Jeeze. What's it about?'

'Secret.'

'Who you gonna sell it to?'

'I don't know.'

'My boyfriend's a writer.'

'Really.'

'He's out of town at the moment. He's at a writers' retreat up in Montana. Say's he's gonna write the Great American Novel.'

'Lucky fellow.'

'Hah. He'd be lucky to write the Great American grocery list. Listen – why don't I give you his agent's number? Maybe he could put you in touch with some people.'

'That'd be marvellous.'

'Come back tomorrow. I'll bring you the number.'

Finalyson rang for the manager when he got back to the motel.

'What?' the manager said, coming out into the lobby, a towel draped round his shoulders.

'How do I operate the cable channels?' Finlayson asked.

'Cable?'

'It says free cable on the sign. I want to see a movie.'

'Oh – a movie. You want to see a movie, huh?'

'Yes.'

'You want to see PUSSY.'

'I beg your pardon?'

'Yeah. You want to see some filthy shit. Teenage pussy. Six guys, one girl. Can't bring yourself to do it yourself, so you have to watch it. Girls with big titties, wavin' their asses on the screen so you could almost reach out and grab 'em with your hand. Let me tell you – we don't cater for that sort of sick shit here. This isn't that kind of motel. Is that clear?'

'Crystal clear. All I had in mind was a movie.'

'I hear it loud and clear all that you had on your mind, pal . . . that much you said. And like *I* said, don't be ringing this bell with such requests in the future. Good day!'

The manager slammed his office door shut.

Finlayson went to his room.

If he didn't have cable, Finlayson thought, all he had to do was say so.

When she saw Finlayson, the waitress approached his table, visibly excited, just short of an all-out run. 'I got you the number,' she said. 'Matt's agent. I spoke to Sid last night. He's a scream. He said, sure, it's fine to give him a ring. Isn't that terrific?'

'That's wonderful,' Finlayson said, taking the slip of paper.

'He told me he might be able to put you in touch with someone. He asked me what the script was about — don't look so worried, I told him it was a big secret. He said, as long as it's not written in French.'

'French?'

'I told him you were from France.'

'Of course. Yes. No, it's not in French.'

'You must let me know how you get on. When you ring him, remind Sid I sent you.' She pointed to her name tag. Becky.

'I shall make a point of it, Becky,' Finlayson said, putting the slip of paper in his pocket.

'Now, what do you want to eat?' Becky asked.

After lunch, Finlayson made a call to the agent. He was busy, but the secretary told him to leave a number. He told her he could be reached at the Bel Air Motel.

That afternoon he sat through a couple of movies at a multiplex cinema.

What total drivel, Finlayson thought once more. When my script reaches the screen, he went on, the projector will explode, the cinema will burn down to the ground. The audience won't know what's hit them. They'll be altogether shell-shocked. They'll stagger out into the daylight and not know what's real, and what isn't.

Finlayson wandered back to the motel, wondering what he might do that evening. He didn't fancy going to a bar, because that would mean making new friends. He was getting tired of that. People were damned friendly out here. It was that old theory: you never knew who might get famous.

He picked up a bottle of gin, some ice and tonic water at the 7-Eleven.

Back at the motel, he fixed a drink and switched on the TV.

What tripe, what dismal drivel . . .

The manager was on the phone in the lobby as Finlayson was going out the next morning.

'Oh good morning, your majesty,' the manager said. 'I am just talking a call for your majesty. Shall I tell him you'll take the call, your royal highness?'

'I will,' Finlayson said, putting down his case and taking the receiver. The manager stood there, scowling at him.

'This Finlayson?' the voice on the phone snapped.

'Correct,' Finlayson said, nodding.

'Becky told me all about the script. She says she loves it, but pardon my French, she don't know shit from shoe polish. I've lined up a meet for you with a friend of mine, Eric Motson. Produced *Beverly Hills Dwarf* so we ain't fuckin' around. You see that movie?'

'I'm not –'

'You know who he's got in his pocket – Gary Hanzen. He could get Hanzen to lens your script. What do you think about that?'

'He could get who to lend me what?'

'To *direct* it. Never mind. You know where Lazenby Pictures is at?'

'I haven't a clue.'

'Listen, speak to Gloria, my secretary – she'll give you the details. One more thing – what's the film about again?'

'Well –'

'Just don't go too heavy on that espionage thing – Tom Clancy-type top secret thing – OK?'

'Fair enough.'

'You don't sound French. You sound New York – you been pullin' Becky's chain?'

'I didn't –'

'Listen – talk to Gloria. Say hi to Eric from me.'

The line went dead.

Finlayson looked over at the manager. He was stood there, sneering. 'Finished?'

'Could I make a call?' Finlayson asked, hanging on to the phone.

'The payphone is down the hall.'

'Have you any change?'

'Jesus, Jessop and Moses!'

'Eric? This is Sidney. Listen – I'm sending over a kid with a script today. Hot property. From Europe.'

'What's the scrip about?'

'He'll tell you about it tomorrow. Put it this way – I started it last night while I was sat on the crapper. I didn't get off the crapper 'til I'd finished it!'

'Big pile of crap, huh? What it is, comedy, tragedy, what?'

'Put it this way, it's so funny it'll make your eyeballs bleed.'

'What happens?'

'All kinds of shit. You go up, you go down, you go back up again.'

'Kind of like a roller-coaster ride, is that it?'

'You bin readin' my mail. Exactly. All kinds of crazy shit.'

'Who do you see in it?'

'Christ almighty, Eric. This is no vehicle picture. Did you think "who do I see in this?" when you came up with *Beverly Hills Dwarf*?'

'This ain't a dwarf picture, is it!? Ever since *Beverly Hills Dwarf*, people sending me nothing but dwarf pictures. You know what I need like a hole in the head? A motherfucking scrip featuring as the lead character a fucking dwarf. Send someone round with a gun to shoot me, right in the fucking head.'

'It's why I'm sending this guy over. This is totally new, and I mean totally new.'

'I'll take your word for it. Send the kid over. If it's a dwarf I'll shit.'

Finlayson sat at the end of a long boardroom table at Lazenby Pictures, the producer, Eric Motson, a mere speck in the distance.

'OK. Don't waste my time, you got five minutes.'

'For what?'

'Crackpot,' Motson murmured. 'The pitch, dummy. Let me have the pitch. That's four minutes.'

'What is that?'

'What's what?'

'The pitch.'

'Where you tell me the plot. In a sentence or two. Three minutes now.'

'I couldn't possibly.'

'You're not going to tell me what it's about?'

'Not in two lines.'

'Three lines, then, whatever.'

Finlayson shook his head.

'What is it called?'

Finlayson looked alarmed. 'Called?'

'Which fucking planet did you recently arrive from? You need a translator? What, pray tell, is the title of the thing?'

'I couldn't tell you that either.'

Motson rubbed his forehead and pushed back his hair. 'What, are you worried I'm going to steal it? Is that it? Is that what this is about again? No one trust me any more?'

'I don't know.'

Motson pointed to a gold-framed poster of *Beverly Hills Dwarf* on the wall.

'Do you know what that is?'

Finlayson regarded it for a moment. 'Well, yes. It's a portrait, silver-framed, of an elf.'

'No, no!' Motson shouted.

'No?'

'That's a title I came up with. A million-dollar title on a hundred-thousand-dollar pic. *Dwarf* just opened where?'

Finlayson shrugged.

'Phili-fucking-ppines. And I don't need to hear anybody say I stole that title. Not some film student who says he brought me the scrip two years ago, July, UCLA film-school grad. Anyone says that again gonna wind up in the boot of a car!' Motson was quite furious now. 'You suggesting I stole the title?'

'Absolutely not.'

'I'm glad. I got foot soldiers on Santa Monica Boulevard. So you'd be wise not to make such a suggestion as this.'

'I'm sorry?'

'Don't be sorry. Tell me who is suggestin' I stole the fucking title of *Beverly Hills Dwarf* that makes you come here today, reluctant to diverge details of your fucking masterwork. You tell me, I slap some fucking respeck into them.'

'I really don't . . .'

'You don't. You don't? So there's no problem. So now – tell me the fucking title of your piece, and briefly synopsise what occurs therein, or get the fuck out of my office.'

Finlayson got up and left quietly.

Motson fell back in his chair, stunned.

'How did the pitch meeting go?' Becky said, approaching Finlayson at his now usual booth in the restaurant.

'I think he was rather intrigued,' Finlayson said.

'That's great,' she said. 'We should go for a drink tonight to celebrate. I'll call Sid. You can tell him how it went. Hell, I bet you haven't been out yet. So busy with all this Hollywood razzamatazz.'

Before he set out that evening, Finlayson looked at himself in the mirror in his motel room. His suit was beginning to look a bit crumpled. Like he said, he didn't want to stay there any longer than he had to.

He took a cab to the address Becky had given him. She was at the bar, drinking a sophisticated drink. She looked a good deal different from how she dressed in the day. She'd rather overdone it, if anything, wearing a cocktail dress and green rock earrings with a matching necklace.

Finlayson got them both drinks. Becky had had a few already.

'You must get lonely being in town on your own,' Becky said.

'There's plenty to keep me occupied,' he told her.

'Jesus – I get lonely, and I live here.'

'How long is your boyfriend away for?'

'God only knows. Says he won't come back until he's finished his book. Good luck to him, he's welcome to it.' She took a slurp of her drink.

'Is he a good writer, your boyfriend?'

'Try asking him that. He never lets me read his stuff any more. I could never understand it, so he'd get crazy and rip it up in front of me. Big deal, I knew he had it backed up on the computer. I'd love to see your script though. Oh – here comes Sidney.'

Sidney was pushing his way towards them at the bar, like a shark through custard.

'What the hell are you playing at, Frenchy?' he asked Finlayson. He turned to Becky. 'I send this wiseass over to see Eric – he only refuses to show him the script. Refused to tell him anything about it. Christ alive! As much as insinuates that Eric stole the title for *Beverly Hills Dwarf* and will do the same for him. Hold a gun to my head, pull the trigger, I'm done.' He turned back to Finlayson. 'There are a thousand hard-luck stories every week in this town. Don't make me part of yours.'

'Have a drink, Sid,' Becky said.

'I can't. You just used up your one and only favour cheque. I suggest you send this guy back in whatever crate he arrived in.'

Sid moved off the way he'd come.

'I thought you said it went OK,' Becky said.

'Obviously not. You know how it is, sometimes you can't read situations.'

'Ahh – to hell with Hollywood. To hell with Sid. He's so rude. I can't believe he was so rude to you –'

'And to you.'

'And to me. You're new in town. How are you expected to know how it works? You were probably too polite. That's it – these Hollywood people, they don't know about politeness. Manners. Let's have another drink, and screw them. Hello, bartender, yes, you, *asshole!*'

They ended up back at Becky's place. Soon she was in just her bra and panties, sprawled on top of Finlayson.

'Won't Matt mind?' Finlayson mumbled.

'To hell with him. Besides, we got an agreement.'

'Swingers?'

'Swingers my ass. The agreement is that I can do what the hell I like. How do I know what he gets up to at that writers' colony? Last time he went, he didn't come back with a book, he came back with a dose. Try publishing that. Gimme a kiss. Gimme one of those French kisses. I've always wanted one of those.' She pushed her mouth on to his, and moved his hands on to her buttocks. But Finlayson was gone.

She tutted and sat back up. She reached to get a cigarette and spied Finlayson's briefcase on the coffee table. She moved over on the couch and spun it round so the locks were facing her. She tried the catches, but sure enough, they didn't budge. She sighed. She was ever so curious to see that script.

'So this guy comes in. Let me describe him to you – he's wearing a suit – a fucking three-piece suit. Talks in a very high-falutin' way. Obviously queer – who isn't, right? He's got his handbag with these little locks on it. Very faggy, you know, gay as can be. So he comes in and kind of perches on the chair like so. Sid sends this guy over – a friend like that, who needs enemies? You know what they say – keep your friends close, keep your enemies closer. Anyway, I say to the guy, what have you got? Gimme the pitch. He says, oh, I don't have a pitch, I don't need a pitch, with this crazy whinnying voice, waving his hand in the air. I say, who the hell do you think you are, Steven Spielberg? He says, who? Who! Can you believe that? I said to him, don't come in here unprepared. I haven't the time. He starts to panic – he leaps out of his chair, says, this scrip in a masterpiece. I said, really, what is it about? Everything and nothing, he tells me. Well, that narrowed it down. I told him, you're boring me, please return from whence you came. Threw a bit of Shakespeare in his direction. He didn't know whether to laugh or cry. Close the door on your way out, I told him.'

'I heard he accused you of ripping off the title for *Beverly Hills Dwarf*.'

Eric twisted his napkin into a tight knot. 'I hope whoever the hell told you that has a good lawyer . . . and a bulletproof jacket.'

'Between you and me, you did steal that title, didn't you?'

Eric erupted. He brought both fists crashing down on the table, sending glasses flying.

'You say that again, as I live and breathe, I'll tear your fucking lungs out.' He brushed off his lap. 'Now, bring my order, and bring me another drink.'

Gloria, drinking her mid-afternoon coffee, answered the phone.

'Hi, Gloria. This is Ted.'

'Aw, hi, Ted. You want to speak to Sid?'

'Don't disturb Sid. Listen, Gloria – I was speaking with Sid last night, and he tells me about a script that he sent over to Lazenby but they passed on it, you happen to have the guy's details?'

'Who was the guy?'

'New guy in town.'

'Oh, the French guy. Now hang on a moment. I think he was staying over at the Bel Air. Motel, not hotel.'

'You got a number?'

'Try information.'

'What the hell do you mean you're moving out?' the manager said. 'You only just got here. What's wrong with this place?'

'Nothing. It's just that I've found somewhere else to stay.'

'I'll get you a room with a waterbed.'

'There's no need.'

'And dirty movies!'

'Really.'

'I have to say, I'm disappointed.'

'Many thanks,' Finlayson said, and walked out the front door.

The manager gazed after him wistfully. 'Fucking son of a bitch,' he said. The phone rang. He snatched it up off the cradle. 'No, he's not here – and I am no longer his fucking answering service. No, I don't know where he went. Matter of fact, I don't give a shit. Somewhere better than this, I suspect, as if such a place exists. Well, it may be important, but I don't know. He just this minute left. Should I run after him for you? Whaddaya mean you'd appreciate it? I was kidding. Hang on. He just walked back in.' The manager put the phone to his chest. 'Ahh – I knew you'd change your mind.'

'I forgot to return my room key,' Finlayson said, putting the key on the counter. The manager looked disappointed.

'Here – a call for you.'

Finlayson took the phone.

'Hello?'

'My name is Ted Rexel. You don't know me. Reason I call is – I'm very interested in seeing the screenplay.'

Finlayson didn't say anything.

'Why don't we meet for lunch?'

'I'd love to,' Finlayson said.

The manager stood there scratching his head.

Finlayson put down his case and looked around the apartment.

'Where am I going to sleep?' he asked.

'In the bed with me,' Becky told him.

'What if your boyfriend comes back?'

'He can sleep in the bed with us. You want some lunch?'

'Actually, I'm meeting someone for lunch.'

'Who?' she asked. He told her. 'I'm impressed,' she said. 'I don't know who that is, but I'm impressed.'

'Order what you like,' Rexel told Finlayson, flipping out the big white napkin on to his lap.

Finlayson took his napkin and tucked it into his collar. He looked at the menu card.

'I don't really know my way around this Los Angeles cuisine.'

Rexel laughed. 'That's good – LA cuisine. Well, just don't get the waiter to recommend anything. Last time I asked, he said, "This is good," and handed me a goddamned script he'd wrote.'

'I suppose you want to hear about my script.'

'Shit, relax. The script can wait. Let's talk about love, life, and mainly, let's talk movies.'

Rexel signalled the waiter.

'You'll never guess what I saw.'

'What?'

'Rexel, with the French guy, having lunch at Les Palmes.'

'No shit! D'you think Rexel is on to something with that guy?'

'It wasn't a social occasion. The waiter didn't bring the phone to his table *once*.'

'What is the script about?'

'It's all very hush-hush.'

'So? What's it about?'

'Well now . . .'

Ted Rexel sat drinking a soda water with another executive from Lazenby Pictures at a bar near their offices.

'So who the hell is this guy and what's he done?' the executive asked.

'Theatre,' Rexel told him.

'Theatre. In Los Angeles?'

'Chrissakes. London – England. Right now, over there – he's –'

'How come I never heard of him?'

'When did you last go to the theatre?'

'I never go to the theatre. I saw my kid's school play.'

'Shit, nobody goes to the theatre. The point is, over there he's a name to be conjured with.'

'He's a fucking magician?'

'In a manner of speaking. He's got something.'

'Script any good?'

'Huh?'

'The script. How is it?'

'It's a thing,' Rexel mumbled.

'What?' the executive asked.

'Ted, this is Jo Gaines from *Movieline* . . . Listen, I'm ready to run this story – something along the lines of "Rexel to pick up spec script by total unknown", so let me know if you're going with it – like I said, if you don't, I'll be talking to someone else, and then you're the guy that didn't.'

Becky dreamed she was walking through the apartment, naked. The briefcase was open on the coffee table, a beam of moonlight illuminating a manila envelope inside the case. She moved towards it and picked up the envelope. There was a wax seal securing the flap of the envelope. She broke the seal and reached inside.

She turned.

Finlayson was standing there, naked, and glistening red from head to toe, eyes blazing yellow. She dropped the envelope.

Finlayson stretched out his arms. 'Let's begin,' he said.

A wall of flame rose up behind him.

'We've got a problem here, Finlayson,' Rexel said.

'What is the problem?'

'You're not letting me see the script.'

'You said yourself you're going to buy it. Why should you need to see it?'

'Why should I – ?' Rexel couldn't answer that. 'Look – I can get Farrell to topline. With Farrell onboard we can get Hanzen to lens.'

'Farrell to top-what?'

'Never mind. I gotta see the *script.*'

'But if I show you, without any guarantee you take it, what's to stop you – ?'

'Taking the idea? It doesn't work like that. People don't steal ideas wholesale. If it's high concept, maybe, but let's hope this thing isn't high concept. High concept is finished. Look, Finlayson, if you're sitting on a hot property, your time is now. Let me look at the script. It's most irregular. This thing should be done through your agent in London anyway. You've got no business selling your own script. It's not how it works.'

'My agent?'

'I know it's not about agents, not about money, it's about art, right? I know about art, I got Tayborn originals hanging on my walls at home. You hear of Tayborn? German guy, beautiful stuff, crazy abstract stuff.'

Finlayson shrugged.

'Don't worry about that. Now, I'd just like to see the script.'

Finlayson got up to leave.

Rexel threw up his arms in despair.

The phone rang as Finlayson left.

'Ted?'

'Yeah.'

'Are you going with *Untitled 38*?'

'Untitled what?'

'Thirty-eight.'

'What's that?'

'You don't even know what it's called? You got first
dibs on the damn thing. Christ, I heard you had the guy
eating crackers out of your hand at Les Palmes the other
day. Because if you're going to pass on the thing, I really
want to get a look at it. I'm only doing this out of
politeness. Rumour has it that Motson is back after it. Can
you believe that? It's your move, Ted.'

Motson picked up the phone in his office.

'Get me the Levene brothers in the office. Send them
right through when they arrive.'

'Remember you have a four o'clock with Dick –'

'Cancel it. I want the Levene brothers here,
immediately.'

Ted rang Finlayson at Becky's apartment.

'How about this, Finlayson. We give you an advance on
the script to look at it with an option to buy and you show
it to no one else around town?'

'How much would this advance be?'

'Name a figure and I'll tell you if you're close.'

'Would it be an awful bother to have cash?'

'You need cash?'

'Well, I don't have a bank here. And I need to set
myself up.'

'Let's see what we can do.'

'I can't sleep on a couch for ever,' Finlayson went on.

Motson had fallen to brooding, swivelled round on his chair, looking at the framed *Beverly Hills Dwarf* poster on the wall. The Levene brothers came in.

'You wanted to see us.'

Motson spun back round and got up. 'Ah yes. I need you to get something for me. There's a guy hawking a scrip round town that I should have had first motherfucking refusal on. He's camped out at the Bel Air. See if you can't get hold of the scrip. Or better still, bring him over here.'

'What does this guy look like?'

'Not like you or I, you know what I'm saying. French, I think. Wears a suit.'

'That's not a problem. Hey – I finally caught up with your dwarf movie on video last night. That's a great fucking movie. The bit where he's tryin' to drive the Rolls-Royce, but can't reach the pedals. Hilarious shit!'

'Like I said, time is of the essence.'

The Levene brothers shuffled out of the office. Motson sat back down. He slammed his hand on the table. I won't just be remembered for the dwarf pic, he thought, I'm damned if I'll let *that* happen.

'What the hell is going on here?'

Matt was standing at the end of the bed.

Becky woke up.

'Who the hell is that?' Matt asked.

'When did you get back?' Becky asked drowsily.

'When does it look like?'

'Did you finish your book?'

'Will you answer my question – who the hell is that? And what is he doing in my bed?'

'That's uh – he just sold his script.'

'No shit.' Matt went over to the bed and grabbed Finlayson's arm that was hanging down the side of the bed.

'HEY, BUDDY – WAKE UP!' he said, shaking Finlayson. 'I said, WAKE UP!'

Finlayson came to, blinking.

'Congratulations, man! That's a hell of a thing. To get sold!'

'I'll make coffee,' Becky said, getting out of bed.

Matt and Finlayson sat in the front room. Matt was strumming a guitar, and talking.

'Shit, you really, nearly, sold your script?'

'Looks that way.'

'That's fucking A, man. Selling it is. If it's sold, it's art. If it's in your drawer, it's just paper.'

'You think so? I mean – what do you write for?' Finlayson asked.

'What publication?'

'No. For what reason, exactly?'

'Name in lights, man, same as all of us. A book with a single fucking name on it, one hundred and fifty thousand words, all my words, making me a wise man.' Twang.

'How's your book coming along?'

'Stalled on the first chapter. Words, man, shit.'

That night they had a party at Becky's apartment to celebrate. Matt seemed the most happy of all, acting like he'd sold the thing.

Even Matt's agent, Sidney, was there, saying half jokingly, 90 per cent serious, 'If this goes through I'll take my 10 per cent.'

The next morning a messenger came round to deliver Finlayson's advance and pick up the script. Finlayson took the script out of his case and replaced it with the money.

'This is the place. Pull in here.'

'Sure?'

'Of course I'm sure. Bel Air *Motel*.'

'I don't want a scene like at the last place.'

'Motson said Bel Air, I assumed —'

'You assumed. I just don't want a scene. I swear that was Denzel Washington walked past when you started throwing shit around.'

'Like hell it was.'

'I swear. I don't want any shit like that here.'

'Like Denzel Washington would stay at *this* dump.'

'You never know. He might be researching a part.'

'What as, a fucking cockroach?'

'Let's go in.'

The Bel Air Motel was all but empty, which was causing the manager some distress. He was thinking of ways he could drum up trade. So far he hadn't thought of any. Maybe changing the wording on the sign would work. At the moment it read 'FREE CABLE — AIR CON — WATERBED'. Which reminded him. He didn't have cable any more. It had been cut off. And the waterbed was leaking and little mushrooms were starting to appear on the carpet and the room smelled awful.

When the Levene brothers came in, eager for them to take up residency, he asked them, 'You want a room, you two guys?'

The brothers, having already been led on a merry dance at the Bel Air Hotel before realising their mistake, were in no mood for fun and games. 'What the fuck are you insinuating? That we were going to book into a room together?'

'Hey, hey, take it easy. To save some money, share a room. That's all. I just thought, with the shaved heads —'

'Again with the cracks. Do we look like we need to save money?' One of the brothers stepped forward and slapped the manager in the face to illustrate the point. The manager howled and stamped his foot.

'We're looking for the guy who's booked in here.'

Rubbing his jaw, the manager asked, 'What guy?'

'Foreigner. Wears a suit.'

'Oh yeah, King of England. He moved out.'

They pulled him on to the counter, then got him round the neck. The manager gurgled and spluttered.

'Now he's making out we're stupid.'

'His registration card. Look in the box there. Under "F". His address in New York.'

One of the Levene brothers picked up the red plastic box and flipped through the cards. He pulled out Finlayson's card and read it.

'Whadsit say?'

He showed his brother the card. It read: *FINLAYSON, Apt 123, Fourth Floor, 567 89th Street, NY.*

'Trying to be funny?'

Ted Rexel opened the envelope and slid out the script.

There wasn't a title or a name or anything on the cover sheet. He flipped through it.

Blank pages.

A couple of hundred of them.

He picked up the phone and rang Finlayson at Becky's.

As the phone rang he thought, yeah, this is part of it. Kind of a publicity stunt. One for the actors to talk about at the press junkets. 'You shoulda seen the first draft.' It was a good one. But Rexel also sensed the first waves of panic. He felt he would very much like to see the script proper, for real, right now.

Someone picked up.

'Hello?'

'Hi, yeah, listen, I need to speak to Finlayson, right away.'

'Finlayson? Oh yeah, Frenchy, hang on.'

The dozy fuck at the end of the line put the phone down and stumbled off into the apartment. Rexel heard him stub his toe on the edge of the sofa and curse. He shouted, 'Hey, Becky, where's Frenchy?' He came back to the phone.

'He's cleared out, man.'

'OK.' Rexel hung up.

Not OK at all. The panic very real now.

The Levene brothers had tortured the motel manager for a while, getting nothing out of him; even when they'd threatened to shave off his beard they'd got nothing out of him, so they went ahead and shaved it off, but still nothing. He had a very strange attitude.

'Listen,' he said, blood bubbling on his lips, 'I want to help, but I can't think of anything. The guy is what we call in the trade a bona fide prick. Awoo! What the hell was that for?'

'Tell us something we can fucking *use*,' one of the Levene brothers shouted at him.

'Screw it,' the other said. 'Let's go.'

They left the manager tied to a chair in his office. As he heard the door slam it came to him.

'Guys,' he cried out, trying to hop the chair towards the door. 'Guys, come back!'

The Levene brothers were halfway across the parking lot when they heard him calling out. They looked at each other. 'This has got to be a joke. He's calling us back in.' They turned around.

The manager was craning his bruised and bloodied head through the door.

'GREYHOUND BUS!' he screeched. 'He came to town on a Greyhound.'

'And?'

'Maybe he bought a return ticket.'

'I don't know where the hell he is. We had a party last night.'

'Sit down and shut up.' Ted Rexel's man pushed Matt down on the couch. 'Mind if I use your phone?'

'Go ahead.'

The man was already dialling. Someone answered fast.

'It's me. We need guys at the airport. Checking planes for New York, London, Europe. You can't miss this guy — white suit, briefcase, name of Finlayson. Get on to this right away. Looks like he's skipping out.'

*

Finlayson was about to board the Greyhound bus when a little guy he'd first encountered on arriving in the city appeared.

'I see you didn't get rich,' the little man said, curling his lip.

'On the contrary,' Finlayson replied, stepping up on to the bus.

'You're a liar,' the little man said.

'Perhaps,' Finlayson said, clutching his briefcase. The engine started and the doors shut. Finlayson took his seat.

The little man stood on the kerb, his hands stuck in his pockets. He watched the bus move off. Then he walked away.

'Sorry, folks, but it's going to get a little hot in here today, seeing as how the air conditioning is not working,' the driver announced over the tannoy. 'We should be arriving in Phoenix, Arizona, in approximately eight hours,' which was where Finlayson was getting off.

Finlayson settled in his seat, and watched through the window as they headed for the city limits. The bus had gone four blocks when the driver stamped on the air brakes, throwing everyone forward. A bad start to an eight-hour journey with no air conditioning.

A black Cadillac had blocked the bus's way on the street.

The Levene brothers forced the doors and boarded the bus.

They worked their way methodically along the aisle, until they saw the character fitting their boss's description, picked him and his case up and dragged him to the car.

Finlayson sat in a crumpled heap in Motson's office once again.

'Open the case,' Motson told one of the Levene brothers.

'It's locked.'

'Just get it open.'

The Levene brother closest to the case grabbed it and squeezed both sides, bursting it open in a shower of money.

'What did Rexel pay you for the scrip?'

Finlayson told him.

'Expensive. But he got a good deal.'

'That was the advance.'

'Advance!' Motson's face lit up. 'Hold on.' He picked up the phone. 'Gloria. Put me through to Anthony.' He winked at Finlayson. 'Anthony – listen. I need to get first refusal on a property but my client took an advance else-where on said property, and now he wants out. So he can bring the thing to me – did he what? – hold on – did you sign anything?'

Finlayson shook his head.

'No. Really? Good.' He hung up. 'I'll double the advance if you bring ME the script.'

'Cash?'

'I'll open the fucking safe right now.' He jumped up and pushed aside the framed poster of *Beverly Hills Dwarf*, revealing a small steel safe built into the wall.

'Fine,' Finlayson said.

'Pick up all that money,' Motson said to the Levene brothers and they got down on their hands and knees.

'When can we see the script, Ted? We're very anxious to get a look at it. *Movieline* want to do a piece on the whole thing. Can you get your man to send a treatment? We don't even know what the damn thing is about.' He laughed in Rexel's ear.

'Absolutely, I'll get on to it.'

'Bring the script over, we can have lunch.'

Rexel noticed another line flashing. Perhaps they'd got hold of 'Frenchy'.

'I'll speak to you later.'

'Will do, Ted.'

Rexel punched the button for the other line.

'Yes?'

'Ted – this is Motson. I got your man here.'

'You have him? Really?'

'I also got some bad news for you.'

'What's that?'

'He's bringing the scrip to us. Don't worry, you'll get your advance back. I'll pay it to you personally. And yes, we can do this, Ted, in fact we are doing it right now. He didn't sign a damn thing. He's signed with us now. The scrip belongs to me.'

'It does?'

'Don't sound so shocked. By rights you shouldn't even have a copy of it.'

'I don't know what to say.'

'It was mine in the first place —'

'Then it's yours again now.'

'I knew you wouldn't give me any shit,' Motson told him, and hung up.

No amount of persuasion would bring Finlayson to avail himself of Motson's private facilities. He had some important business back in New York to which he had to attend. He'd be in touch with Motson about rewrites.

'I'll have my limo drive you to the airport.'

'I'll get a cab.'

'What is it with you? Live a little. You're in Hollywood now. Take the limo – champagne, cigars. I'll get one of my girls to ride with you, suck your dick in the back seat.'

'No really, I'll take a cab.'

He took a cab to the train station, where he got a train to San Diego, and then a tram to the Mexican border.

*

Motson was on the phone to Rexel once more.

'Did you read it yet?' Motson asked.

'What?'

'The scrip. *My* scrip.'

'Not exactly.'

'But you know what's in it?'

'In a manner of speaking.'

'But you sent it over just now?'

'It's on its way.'

'OK. The suspense is killing me. You gotta put me out of my misery. Tell me – tell me, tell me there ain't any dwarves in the damn thing.'

'None at all,' Rexel said.

'Thank God,' Motson said.

FIN

shandoman redux

When Putzo and his vile hordes threatened to invade the city, the Mayor put out the call for Shandoman. The Shando-sign – a snaking yellow 'S' shape – lit up the city sky.

Shando's aide-de-camp, Russell, entered Shandoman's study in his mansion on the outskirts of the city. Shandoman sat in front of the fireplace, his head hanging forward, gazing into the flames.

'Shandoman,' Russell said. 'Have you seen the –'
'The sign? Yes, I've seen it.'
'Shall I – prepare the Shandomobile?' Russell said.
Shandoman turned his head to look at Russell.
'That won't be necessary.'
'What? You mean – you're going on foot?'

'I'm not. I won't be going — at all,' Shandoman said, and looked back towards the fire.

'But — you must.'

Shandoman shook his head.

'Why, Shandoman, why? When the city is relying on you!'

'I'll tell you,' Shandoman said.

The Mayor sat in his office, yelling into the phone.

'What do you mean he hasn't got back to us? You put the Shando-sign in the sky, and nothing? Well, keep trying, keep trying. They might attack tonight, for God's sake. In the meantime, mobilise all our troops, and the police force. I know, I know, but it's the best we can do until Shandoman arrives.' A light started flashing on the phone. 'Look, I have to go, I have another call. It might be him.' He flicked the button on the phone.

'Shandoman? Is that — oh, it's *you*. I thought I might hear from YOU, Putzo. You heard what? Well, you heard wrong. Shandoman's fine and he's coming. When? That would be telling. You take your chances, Putzo. Why is the Shando-sign still lit up? To remind *you*, Putzo, to remind you he's *coming*. What? . . . well, you do that, Putzo, you do that, you take out the city's main power supply, knock yourself out, yes, feel free, see how far you get. You want to what? — set fire to the . . . well, yes, be my guest, that's fine, you go right ahead, who needs City Hall? Yes, uh-huh, right. What!' The Mayor scowled and started pointing into the mouthpiece of the phone. 'Now listen here, Putzo – you leave my wife out of this . . . I draw the line at that disgusting talk! You try that and – and –' The Mayor slammed down the phone and swivelled round in his chair to look out towards the Shando-sign projected above the skyline.

'Come on, Shandoman – we're relying on you.'

The doctor was checking Shandoman's blood pressure.

'How do you think you got to feeling this way?'

'Just recently things have been mounting up. All this talk of Putzo. Everything seems to have got on top of me. I know it's just a state of mind, doctor – the waves, the dark waves – it's irrational, but I can't stop it. Once I take the medication I'll be OK, won't I?'

'We know these worked for you before, Shandoman, so there's no reason why they shouldn't work for you again.'

'Thank you, doctor. Will they take effect quicker this time, seeing as I have used them before?'

'I'm afraid they'll will take up to two weeks to be effective.'

'Two weeks! That's no good. Putzo could attack at any time – I need to be better – I can't afford to feel like this. I feel helpless, desperate, oh!'

'There is no pill that will make you feel better straight away.'

'We've colonised Mars, built cities underwater, invented a time machine —'

'They invented a time machine?' the doctor asked.

'It didn't work but it *nearly* worked.'

'I didn't hear about that.'

'I read about it. In a magazine in your waiting room. All this and they can't come up with a cure for depression that doesn't take half a month to work. Why, I ask you, why, *why*?'

'You're becoming mildly hysterical, Shandoman. You'll just have to forget about Putzo, and concentrate on getting yourself better.'

'Forget about Putzo?!'

'If you like, I can write you a sick note.'

'Oh no, I'm finished, finished, you hear!'

'You must try and relax. Your blood pressure is up. I'm going to give you something to help you sleep.'

'Finished,' Shandoman said, his voice trailing off.

Putzo had two of his men hijack an airliner and crash it into the city's main power supply. He sent a message to the Mayor that stated, simply, 'FOR STARTERS'.

The Mayor stared down at the city. He could see flames rising in the east quarter. In the distance he could make out the domed roof of the Colosseum disintegrating like an eggshell; and to the left of that, the Loomis Sports Stadium was a green glow of fire – they'd only reopened that three months ago. The city was in a state of emergency. He tugged at his hair.

'Where the hell is he, where the *hell* is Shandoman? Goddammit!' He beat his fists against the window sill. This is not like him, he thought, not like him at all. Right when we need him the most. Right when we need him more than ever. He's never let us down before.

He leaned back and chewed his lips and thought . . . not like him . . . of course, not like him . . . that was it. A trick! Part of his plan. Putzo would be expecting him to come – and Shandoman was simply avoiding Putzo's trap – the counter-bluff! Yes, surely that was it. Shandoman hadn't told the Mayor, hadn't told anyone, to ensure his plan was highly effective. Devious!

The Mayor grinned. Bring your guns, bring your knives, Putzo, we're waiting! he thought. 'Good ol' Shandoman,' he said, giggling, rubbing his hands together. 'I knew we could rely on him.'

He put a call through to Russell at the Shando-mansion. 'Tee-hee, Russell, I know all about it.'

'You know? About what? How – his doctor?'

'What has his doctor got to do with this? Is he ill?'

'Well, in a manner of speaking –'

'Aha – yes – of course – ill, eh? Yes, yes, that's a good ruse! So when can we expect him?'

'You can't rush these things – the medication –'

'Medication — ha ha, I understand, yes. Attention to detail. Pull the wool over Putzo's eyes.'

'This is no laughing matter, Mayor.'

'No, not at all. Well, we'll be here — waiting. Send Shandoman my "best wishes".'

The Mayor hung up the phone. Good ol' Shandoman! Pretending to be incapacitated, while all the time he was setting his own trap to take Putzo down, hook, line and sinker! The Major couldn't have planned it better himself.

Shandoman took his second pill. He'd sunk into a terrible gloom. In thirteen days he would be better. Thirteen days! Thirteen days was a lifetime, and whatever way he calculated it, it was still thirteen days.

The Mayor was in his office the next morning. Russell had telephoned him.

'Hit me with it,' he said.

'He's not coming —'

'Why, for God's sake, why —'

'He can't.'

'Cuh — *can't*?'

'Not yet.'

'For God's sake, when? We need him now!'

Russell explained the grim news.

This is part of the ploy, surely, the Mayor thought, only slightly dubious.

*

Russell brought in the morning papers on a silver tray.

He put them by Shandoman's bed and went to draw the curtains.

'Leave them!' Shandoman snapped. He didn't want to see the smoke from the smouldering city through the windows. He peered at the headline on the paper. 'PUTZO DESTROYS –' was all he could read. He pushed the papers on to the floor.

'Will you be requiring the Shandomobile today?' Russell asked.

'No, I shall not,' Shandoman said, trying to muster some quiet dignity, and buried his head in the pillows.

'Remember to take your pill,' Russell said.

'I won't forget *that*,' Shandoman said. 'Please leave.'

Shandoman took his pill. 'I must be strong,' he said to himself.

The Mayor held a press conference.

'How can you explain Shandoman's no-show to the citizens?' asked George Ryan from the *City Star Chronicle*.

'Shandoman's had a breakdown –' the Mayor blurted out.

'A breakdown!' Adrian Peterson from the *Times Herald Reporter* cried out. The room was in uproar, the press corps jumping up out of their seats, throwing their notepads in the air.

'Please, stay calm,' the Mayor's adviser said. 'What the Mayor means to say is that the Shandomobile – *broke down* – yes, that's it – on his way to the city – plain conked out.'

'Can they fix it?' asked Marcus Weaver from the *Courier Despatch*.

'They're working on it,' the Mayor said.

'How soon?' Weaver persisted.

'Well, they need a new part – that has to be shipped in.'

'What part?' said Owen Fields from the *Late Edition*.

The Mayor leaned across to his adviser, who whispered something in his ear. 'The flux capacitator,' the Mayor said.

'Anything else?' Owen continued.

'Some flanges,' the Mayor said.

'What are flanges?' asked Ben Wallis from the *Union Times*.

'How the hell should I know? Do I look like a mechanic? If I was, I'd roll my sleeves up and get over there and pitch in as best I could! Any more questions?' the Mayor asked, impatiently.

'Do you believe that the city will be saved?' asked Dave Gaffney from the *New Republic Gazette*.

'There's no doubt in my mind it will happen.'

'In the meantime,' asked Frank Joseph from the *Metropolitan Evening News*, 'what is being done to prevent Putzo from killing innocent citizens?'

'Everything in our capacity,' the Mayor said. 'But I will admit – we need Shandoman. I wish he were here now.'

The pressmen murmured in agreement and filtered out to file their copy.

As if in answer to the Mayor's wish, over at the Shando-mansion, Shandoman came striding purposefully out of his room, nearly tripping over Russell in the hallway.

'Bring me my Shando-suit,' he said, 'and start up the Shandomobile!'

'YES, SIR!' Russell said.

The gates of the Shando-mansion opened and there was a rumbling noise. Suddenly, the Shandomobile came tearing out and veered left, spraying gravel and leaving a trail of dust as it headed towards the city; sleek, red, fast, deadly.

Five hundred yards down the road it screeched to a halt.

'No – can't – too soon – not ready,' Shandoman said.

'You'll have to drive us back,' he said to Russell, and got out of the driver's seat.

Putzo and his hordes wreaked more and more havoc, marching through the streets with a crude effigy of Shandoman which they set on fire atop the Memorial Plaza in the city's central square.

*

The Mayor could barely sleep and when he did, he had nightmares, Putzo leering over him, his fangs dripping. The Mayor would wake screaming, the bed soaked with sweat.

'Must – be – patient,' Shandoman said, rocking backwards and forwards in the chair, trying to calm himself, until the doctor arrived.

The doctor had called earlier, saying he had some news that might be of interest.

'What is it?' Shandoman asked him as he came in.

'Fellow by the name of Kinsley. Invented a device. Very much at the experimental stage at the moment.'

'What's it do?'

'It provides an instantaneous reaction – a cure if you like – which rids the mind of depression, just like that. Incredible really.'

'Does it work?'

'Well, the results so far have been pretty positive. He's tried it on animals – dogs and so forth –'

'Dogs get depressed?'

'Oh yes.'

'What is this guy, a vet?'

'No, no. He's tested a couple of people also, mild depressives. Now, if you want to go ahead and try this, you'd have to sign a waiver form for liability. Not that it's unsafe, but as I said –'

'When can I do it?'

'Any time. Luckily the clinic is outside of the city limit. God knows, it might well have been blown to pieces by Putzo by now if it —'

'I don't want to hear about that!' Shandoman snapped.

The doctor arranged for Shandoman to visit the Kinsley clinic the very next morning. Shandoman signed the waiver and was led through to Kinsley's consulting rooms.

'The effects, so far, are very good, very good,' Kinsley said, looking at the waiver form, then folding it and putting it in his jacket pocket. 'My life's work — near complete, in this single machine,' he said, pointing to a cylindrical device with a perspex door. 'It takes the negative impulses from here —' he pointed to Shandoman's head — 'and transfers them there.' He pointed to the machine.

'How quickly does it work?'

'Immediately.'

'My God.'

'How bad do you feel?'

'Very bad.'

'Good. Excellent. Let us try.'

Shandoman was strapped to a reclining chair, wires attached to a band around his head.

'All we need now is a receptacle to absorb the negative energy,' Kinsley said. He went over to the corner of the room and picked up a potted plant. 'Here, you see — a healthy house plant. Ha! Never trust a doctor whose house plants are dead! Alive, you see, an organism.' He opened the perspex door to the machine, put the plant inside the chamber and shut the door.

'Now we are ready. Soon you will feel much better – in just a moment, because of this machine – the only one of its kind – my life's work, right here!'

Kinsley threw a lever on the side of the machine. It began to hum. Shandoman felt the band tighten around his head. The plant wilted and the door blew off its hinges. The circuit board on the side of the machine caught fire, there was a loud bang and the contraption exploded and disappeared in a cloud of smoke. When the smoke cleared, it was in pieces all over the floor.

'Oh my God!' Kinsley cried out, falling to his knees, sobbing.

'Sorry,' Shandoman said.

The only paper still up and running – the *Student New Journal* – was starting to print increasingly sceptical editorials about Shandoman failing the city. On the advice of his adviser, the Mayor called another press conference.

Eager young student journalist Dimitri Paltrow fired off his first question: 'What can you do to quash the rumours that Shandoman is suffering from depression?'

The Mayor looked startled. 'Where did you hear about this?'

Dimitri shrugged coyly. 'A journalist never reveals his sources,' he said.

The Mayor's assistant whispered in his ear. The Mayor straightened up. 'Whatever the rumour, you heard it wrong,' the Mayor said. 'It's not "depression", it's "dee pressure" – the pressure.'

'He's suffering from the pressure? What does that mean? He can't take the pressure?'

'No, no, he thrives on pressure.'

Dimitri dutifully scribbled this on his notepad. 'So why isn't he doing anything?'

'I can't tell you that.'

'The public has a right to know.'

'And if the public know – so will Putzo. We don't want to play into his hands.'

'Well, actually only students will know. Those that bother to read the paper,' Dimitri mumbled sulkily. 'It's not like they have to pay for it.'

'Off the record,' the Major continued, 'Shandoman is plotting a trap.'

'What kind of trap?'

'That would be telling.'

'When?'

'When what? When will I tell you?'

'When will he spring the trap?'

'Soon.' Make it soon, the Mayor thought.

Dimitri got up to leave.

'Oh, Dimitri,' the Mayor said. 'When is this coming out?'

'Next week's edition, I think.'

'Make sure you send me a copy.'

Just then, there was an explosion outside on the street and they all fell to the carpet instinctively.

Shandoman had retreated to his mansion, despondent. There were no miracle cures. It was back to the pills.

Russell wanted to update him on what was happening in the city, but Shandoman told him he did not care to hear any more news reports.

Shandoman slept and dreamed that Putzo's men had got hold of him and were parading him through the city streets, tossing him up in the air. He woke with a start, drenched in sweat, his heart beating violently.

'PUTZO!' he cried out, that the fiend might hear him.

After a couple of nights, Shandoman was beginning to sleep better, but still spent the days walking around in a daze, trying not to think about anything. Much as Russell wanted to, Shandoman forbade him from saying what was happening in the city regarding Putzo and his men, lest it hinder his recovery. 'It is better I know nothing about it until I am better, then I can make things better,' he said to Russell.

Shandoman took to sleeping a good deal of the time,

feeling his body restoring itself, and his mind relaxing. He'd been overdoing it, that was all, to the point where he'd become panic-stricken and depressed. That did not do a man any good. But he felt himself getting better – the black waves further apart now – slowly, but surely.

Russell seemed agitated, but Shandoman said, 'Do not worry – I am getting there. You know – I thought I would never feel better again, but now I truly believe there is a light at the end of the tunnel.'

Shandoman opened the French windows that led out into the garden at the back of the mansion. He walked out, and, although it was overcast and grey, he could take some joy in what he saw, where before he might only have felt bleak despair. The deep green of the grass, the tiny white butterflies dancing in the air, the smell of wood burning somewhere. The possibility of happiness did exist, he thought. One more day! Give me one more day!

It was morning. Putzo led his hordes down Main Street, the grey Marcoli architecture looming high on either side. The hordes cheered, overturned trams, broke windows, set things alight and tossed grenades. 'Here we are, fellows, here we are,' Putzo said as they reached City Hall. He stared up at the building – its grand pillars and abutments, the splendid, tall windows, the winged cherubs and carved floral embellishments. Putzo grinned, baring his warthog-like fangs.

*

The Mayor crawled underneath his desk as he heard the door splintering under another axe blow.

'For God's sake, Putzo, back off! I have men in here.'

'You've got nothing in there,' Putzo growled. 'We're coming in, and what we do to you when we get hold of you, well, I don't wanna tell you, in case you faint. I want you to be awake for what we got in store!'

'I'm telling you, Putzo – you've gone too far this time. There will be hell to pay when Shandoman arrives.'

'Don't talk to me about that flake. He ain't coming. You know what I heard – I heard he had a nervous collapse. How about that! This is our scene now, Mayor, and you know it, so you might as well hand us the keys to the city and be done with it.'

'NEVER!' the Mayor cried out, crawling further under the desk. 'Shandoman is coming!'

Putzo's lips curled into a crude grin, visible through the crack in the door. 'Yeah – he's coming all right – apart at the seams!'

There was a tremendous thud as the doors gave way.

Shandoman's eyes flickered open.

He waited a second, to make sure he was not mistaken.

'At last,' he said quietly. 'At last.'

He took a pill from the tray on his bedside and

swallowed it down with a sip of water. He got up out of bed, stretched, then walked through to his dressing room where Russell had hung his clothes. He strapped himself into his Shando-suit. He tightened his Shando-gauntlets and did up his Shando-belt. He clicked his silver Shando-boots together, and checked his Shando-shooter was fully charged. It was.

Shandoman moved over to the intercom on the wall by the door. He pressed the green button.

'Russell,' he spoke into the receiver.

'Shandoman!' Russell said. 'You're better!'

'Let's roll,' Shandoman said. He moved towards the Shando-elevator.

The gates to the Shando-mansion opened. The Shando-mobile came roaring out. In the blink of an eye, it had disappeared, on its way to the city, Shandoman at the wheel.

The Shandomobile moved slowly through the streets.

People lay dead on the pavement. Buildings levelled, gutted, destroyed. The city was a pile of rubble.

'Putzo and his men,' Russell said, shaking his head.

'Let's find Putzo,' Shandoman said. 'Let's put an end to this!'

'It's over,' Russell said. 'They've done what they needed to do, and now they've gone.'

'Ahh shit,' Shandoman said. 'Just when I was ready to kick some Putzo ass!'

The Shandomobile drove on through the demolished city.

hollywood by sundown

Tom Mix took a bullet in the chest and fell down dead in the dirt. There was a ripple of applause and the audience slowly dispersed.

Joe Johnson, who was performing as Wyatt Earp, stood over Mix, who was still playing dead, and said, 'Tom, there's a call for you.'

Mix had taken the call and made his decision, then gathered his men together. 'You guys can carry on without me,' Mix said.

'Without you?' Johnson said. 'It's the *Tom Mix* Wild West Roadshow!'

'People just want shooting and fighting,' Mix said.

'People's want their money back when they realise you're not part of the show,' Peter Fanducci, who played Frank James, interjected.

'Listen,' Mix said. 'I have to do this.' The performers shrugged and muttered. 'I really do.'

Mix hefted his two heavy red buckskin suitcases with copper clasps into the back of his one-seater sports car. He jammed them down behind the seat, got in and started the engine. One suitcase contained his cowboy boots, revolvers, sheriff badges, leather whips, ropes and holsters, the other his fancy embroidered shirts and cowboy suits, silk bandannas and belts. Tucked in behind them, the beautiful Brydon Brothers tan and sterling-silver saddle with bronze rivets and bevelled tassels and gold inlay that his beloved Tony the Wonder Horse used to wear. Rumour had it that when Tony had died Mix had cut off his tail and had it installed as a bedside bell pull in his Hollywood mansion. Mix had laughed off that rumour just the way he had the one that the reason he'd been booted out of Hollywood when the talkies came in was because he had a squeaky voice (another falsehood), the result of a shrapnel wound when he was serving as an artilleryman in the Spanish-American war – or that the squeaky voice was from when he was working as a ranch hand and a horse he was breaking in hoofed him in the throat. That this was the reason they didn't even use Mix's own voice in the *Tom Mix Radio Show*, but an *impersonator's*! People could think what they liked. Mix pointed the car west and headed off.

*

He was heading back to Hollywood – Hollywood, the town that had made him, and the town that had spurned him. He was heading back there now to star in his first ever sound Western – *Comanche Corral* – a script he'd written himself. He'd been run out of town when the talkies arrived and interest in Westerns had died down a little. Hell, audiences wanted to hear people singing – goddam Al Jolson. Was that any way to treat Tom Mix, dandy-dressing cowboy who directed his own movies, did his own stunts, heck, the whole shebang? But now they'd come to their senses, Mix being asked to return when they realised there was no reason that just because Mix couldn't speak back then didn't mean he couldn't talk *now* . . . some bright spark remembered Mix had *star quality*. Mix could hear it now – the sound of hooves on hard dirt, gunshots, Injuns howling and whooping. The audience'd think there were a bunch of Comanches right there in the movie house wanting to scalp them and they'd run clear for the fire doors. Mix drove on.

Mix had thought his career was over, that his card had been punched. He'd been on the verge of signing another deal to tour with his Wild West Roadshow – visiting hick towns and recreating great moments of the frontier days; Custer's last stand and the shoot-out at the OK Corral and so on. It was a step down from the movies but it was work, and he'd needed work after losing most all his money in the great stock-market crash. Then Lou Selig had called and said, 'Mix, get your ass back to Hollywood, pronto!' Selig, who had first met Mix all those years ago when he'd been working at Ranch 101, had said to Mix, 'You sure can handle those horses,' and Mix's fate was sealed. And now Selig was asking him out to Hollywood again. He hadn't needed to be asked twice but he decided to play it out.

'To what do I owe the goddam pleasure, Lou?' he'd said. 'Al Jolson's make-up rub off or something?'

'Listen, Tom, I won't bullshit you. We made a mistake. We could use you here. I read your script and we're going to make it.'

'What are the terms?'

'Get here damn quick, Tom, that's all. People change their minds all the time. Just get to Hollywood, now.'

'Lou, I'm there,' Mix said, then hung up the phone.

A town like Hollywood needed a man like Tom Mix. And Tom Mix needed a town like Hollywood.

He started giving some thought to *Comanche Corral*. In it, a trio of cowboys herding cattle across Texas are attacked by a band of Comanches who lay siege to the ranch the cowboys had planned to stop over in for one night only. The cowboys were on their way to meet a powerful cattle baron who wouldn't wait; if they didn't get there in time, he'd buy other stock, and they'd have made their journey for nothing. But first they had the Comanches to deal with . . .

Just outside of Tuscon, Arizona, Mix pulled into a gas station and told the Mexican attendant to fill the car up.

'Best tek it easy up ahead,' the Mexican said, putting the nozzle into the gas tank. 'Bridge is out.'

'Gotta be in Hollywood by sundown,' Mix told him. He paid the man and drove off.

The desert wind was cool, and the sun hung lazy orange in the sky. He leaned back in his seat, his arm slung over the side of the door, the letters 'TM' embroidered on the sleeve of his hand-stitched red-chequered pearl-buttoned shirt, and gave the accelerator some weight. Mix had Hollywood on his mind. The house in the hills. When people asked him what was the best thing about his job, about being 'famous', he would say, the house in the hills. Sure beat touring in the desert with the roadshow. Mix recalled a pool party he'd had – that had been what might be referred to as a 'swell time'. The booze had run free, the sun had refused to stop shining. Mix had climbed up on to the roof with a good gal he had the yen for – maybe she'd be wife number four – and they had stood there looking out over Laurel Canyon. 'Jesus H,' Mix had said. 'I just can't believe my luck in this town. First I get to handle the horses for a living and someone pays me to do that! Then I get to train 'em, ride 'em, save the girl and shoot the bad guy and hunt bears and kill wolves and I get paid to do *that*.' Not bad for an Oklahoma boy who'd grown up with an outside privvy, and who was now sitting pretty high in the hills on $10,000 a week. He had felt terrible good just then, and sucked down the drink in his hand very fast. He turned to the woman and took a long hard look. 'Nope,' he said. 'I cannot believe my luck.' His luck had run out when the talkies arrived, but now he was being tossed a second chance.

Mix was so occupied with these fine thoughts he missed the first two signs indicating that the bridge was out ahead. The road curved sharply up ahead into a long, wide corner, and Mix didn't see the final 'BRIDGE OUT' sign, and approached the impasse where the road straightened out at some fair lick. Just in good time he realised the busted ridge of concrete rearing up and the deep gorge beyond it and swung the wheel so the car veered hard left off the road, skittering along the verge and spraying gravel. He slammed on the brakes and the car came to a halt, one of the heavy buckskin cases came sliding fast over the top of the single seat and snapped Tom Mix's neck.

Mix was found dead in the ditch and the dust and the weeds the next morning, slumped in his car, his head crushed against the steering wheel, surrounded by the cowboy paraphernalia of his silent-movie days. There was a sheriff badge on the dash; a cowboy boot had gone through the windshield; Tony the Wonder Horse's saddle unceremoniously upturned in the prickles of a cactus. A small lizard sat on a fencepost nearby, sunning itself, while in Hollywood a producer wrung his hands.

the lever

I was having trouble finding someone for the job. It was the time of year I guess, the season of goodwill. Everyone seemed to be in a damned charitable mood. It wasn't like I could arrange the timing of these things, so if it fell two nights before Christmas, so be it, there was nothing I could do about that, short of some kind of a reprieve. And that seemed highly unlikely given the circumstances.

The way it works, and this is strictly off the record – you'll never hear this *officially*, no, sir, not from the horse's mouth, nothing – is that I – that is whoever the task is delegated to – approach someone on the street – God's honest truth, anyone who seems 'suitable' for the role – and offer them four hundred bucks, stone-cold cash, to do the job. Four hundred bucks, and it's not even a day's work – four hundred for an hour, tax-free, no comebacks, completely anonymous. We don't even take their name. But like I say, this time of year, and I picked the short straw to find the man to do the job. Christmas, and suddenly it's goodwill to all men – why it can't be like that the year round I don't know, then maybe we'd never get in this position in the first place. To hell with Christmas, everything shuts down, and for what? Who needs it? Not me, Mac, it was downright inconvenient.

Anyway, I'd asked left, right and centre, I'd gone up and down Main Street, into the bars and pool halls and bus depots, looking for roughnecks in need of some scratch, and nothing. Either people thought I was kidding, or'd turn white and back off. Some even got a little heavy, with all the 'what d'you take me for?' patter. And still I didn't get a bite.

It was getting closer to the time and I still hadn't found anyone, but was telling those who needed to know that it was all 'under control'; it's late one night and I've spent a fruitless day trawling the town, it's too damned cold to be mooching around on a dead trail, and I'm considering casting my net a bit wider, when a door swings open near into my face, and some bum is slung out into the slush on the sidewalk, both him and the slinger shouting abuse at one another, the slinger along the lines of 'and don't think you're gettin' served in here any more!', the bum more in the manner of 'furghnner furnerr –' before he hits the deck.

I move in and help the chump up – he's wearing a dark blue blazer jacket and mismatched pants, smells of a five-day sideswipe and looks up at me as a benevolent friend, his tongue lolling out of his mouth. 'Let's you and me have a drink, Mac,' I say, and hoick him up off the floor.

We're sitting at Barney's, nice and quiet in there, Barney playing goddamned Christmas carols, me drinking a black coffee, him drinking a black coffee with a side-order shot, drying off and warming up.

'You want me to do what?' he says, the mist starting to clear.

I tell him again, briefly. Well, it doesn't take much explaining.

'For how much?'

'Four hundred bucks.'

He knits his eyebrows and scratches his chin, trying to make out he is thinking hard about the proposition, but he wasn't figuring the job at all, just eyeing the shot glass and considering how much hooch that piece of dough would see him to – through Christmas and well out the other side, at the very least. He would have a swell time on the proceeds, if he could stomach the gig. But the way he was socking them back, I guessed he had a strong stomach. Sure, the warning bells rang – they'd told me 'no bums, no lushes' – they're unreliable at the best of times. Who then? A solid upstanding citizen? Sure, they were queuing round the block for a little arm-work like this. I was in a hole, time was running out, and I had a feeling this guy was keen – heck, he'd get so pickled on pay day he'd come to and think it had all been a dream. If he did go for it, I'd tell him to freshen up for a couple of days, and do the job clean. After that, it was his party.

Some people ask, why don't you do the job yourself if it's that simple? Good question. Reason being, how would it look if this kind of work was on the job description? – I'm in the employ of the state after all. It wouldn't look good. This way, it's anonymous. If, some years down the line, you were to ask me who did what to whom, I wouldn't be able to tell you. That's better for everyone.

The bum had quit figuring how long his beer bust was going to run.

'I'll do it,' he said, managing something along the lines of enthusiasm.

'OK,' I said. I talked him through what he had to do, where he had to be, and when. 'And buddy,' I said, 'get yourself cleaned up.'

'Well, see, that's a problem, brother,' he told me. 'If you could see your way clear to an advance on my wages, I might be able to get a room and a shave.'

I pulled out my wallet and pushed a twenty across towards him. 'Use it for what you said, Mac. I don't want you turning up juiced or you and me are the ones for the high jump.'

He nodded and pocketed the note. I knew he'd spend the money on getting soused. Whatever gets you through.

Two days later he came in through the side door like I'd told him. Sure enough, he was wearing the same grubby outfit, bleary-eyed. Hopped to high heaven no doubt. He'd probably had an attack of the jitters – who wouldn't? I should have known better, but like I said, I'd been in a corner. He staggered towards me, blinking in recognition.

'What happened to the clean-up?' I asked him.

'I got rolled that night – I –'

'Save it. You ready for this?' He nodded unconvincingly. I took him up the steps to sign him through. They patted him down and found a half-pint bottle of rotgut tucked in his sock; he shrugged as if to say, 'What did you expect?'

We sat and waited.

'You know what?' he said.

'What?'

'I never did anything like this before.'

'No kidding. You OK with it?'

'I guess so,' he said. He seemed awful pale and shaky. Understandable.

The door opened and we were called through.

'Gonna puke,' he mumbled as we went along the corridor.

'What?'

'Need to puke!'

'Oh Christ – in there.' He headed towards the door.

'I thought you said you were OK with this.'

'Never done this before,' he said, hurrying into the latrine.

When he came back out I nearly didn't recognise him. He was wearing a dirty Santa Claus hat, red with a grey fur trim and the bobble missing, and a Santa beard with an elastic strap. He had a length of tinsel wrapped round his neck and draped down his front.

'What the hell are you playing at?' I said, pushing him against the wall.

'Do you think it would be inappropriate?' he slurred. 'I thought I'd wear it when I did the thing.'

'Why would you do that?'

'For one thing, just to cheer people up, doing it at this time of year and all. And another –' he held out the beard – 'so people don't recognise me! Hell, I don't want someone walking down the street and pointing me out!' He let the beard snap back into place.

'Goddammit!' I said. 'No one needs cheering up, and no one'll see you – they'll be too busy watching the main event. Gimme that stuff.'

I took the hat and the beard and the tinsel and shoved it in my pocket. 'Come on. We gotta go in.'

Everything was going fine, but it doesn't matter how fine everything is going if it doesn't go fine right until the end.

It was right after the reverend had done his bit. My boy's cue. He stepped up, yeah, he managed that. He stepped up, then he caved, sure he did, collapsing and crying out, 'I can't do it, I just can't do it!' I tried to lift him up off the floor, the way I did when I first ran into this sorry case, all the while that warden Brenton eyeing me, making me doubly anxious because he is, by all accounts, one mean-tempered bastard.

'Jesus, man, get a hold of yourself,' I said to the bum.

'That poor man, that poor man!' he wailed. 'God have mercy!'

'Poor man nothing!' I hissed into his ear.

'I knew I shouldn't have been drinking gin. It makes me weepy,' he moaned.

'You're making *me* weepy. Throw the switch.'

It was no use, his whole body went limp. It was hopeless.

'There a problem here?' Brenton said. 'Is this man drunk?'

'No, no, it's fine,' I said, dragging the bum upright and trying to lean him against the wall.

'I smell it on him.' Brenton, quick as a flash, pulled out a blackjack and socked the drunk, who tilted and slid back down like the *Titanic*. 'Get him the hell out of here,' Brenton said to two guards, then turned to me. 'This is your shit,' he said.

*

Brenton made me throw the lever myself. It was unorthodox, certainly, but I didn't have a choice in the matter. 'People have come a long way to see this, and I won't have them go home disappointed,' Brenton said.

If I put it in perspective, though, I didn't feel so bad about it; the guy in the chair was a child-killer, name of 'Chipmunk', and anyone who read anything about what he'd done would agree he deserved to fry. The things he had done to those boys – a few thousand volts was too good for *him*. Incidentally, I got to keep the four hundred bucks, which means it's not going to be such a bad Christmas after all.

piccadilly hustle

Eddie Constantine adjusted his eyepatch, wiping some sweat away from underneath his eye. It got itchy in this hot weather. The patch wasn't a gimmick, even though it might have looked that way — he'd lost his eye a year before as a result of a very rude incident with a knife. He didn't like to talk about it, unless asked, by a prospect maybe, in which case he would spin a yarn wherein he was the victim of a cruel attack. They liked that, it engendered trust.

They came to him like flies, especially on a hot day like this, the pavements crowded, and he in his light blue linen suit leaning nonchalantly against the railings on Shaftesbury Avenue, just along from Piccadilly Circus, giving him a respite from the bloody crowds. He'd thought of a glass eye, but that was in fact more sinister than an eyepatch; you could match the colour of the eye, but the glass eyeball didn't move in at all, it just looked *dead*.

He was lighting a cigarette when a tall, crew-cut man wearing a green T-shirt, dragging a grey Samsonite, came over to him. A woman stood on the pavement behind the man, holding on to the handle of her suitcase. People pulling their whole lives around with them in those fucking suitcases, Eddie thought . . .

'Excuse me, can you tell me where Sherwood Street is?' the man asked.

It was just Constantine's luck that some bright spark had opened a hostel on Sherwood Street, right in the thick of it but nearly impossible to find. A blip of a street on the map, not two minutes' walk away from Piccadilly but which might as well be two hundred miles away if you didn't know how to find it. And panic set in easy in Piccadilly – bright lights, big shithole – get me the hell out of here, get me to my *room*.

'Sherwood Street,' Eddie said, ruminating.

'We look for the hostel there.'

'The hostel. Yeah, sure, I'll show you myself.'

The big man motioned to his partner, and the three of them stood at the kerb, waiting to cross. The light turned red and they started to walk, the couple following Eddie, the Pied Piper of Piccadilly.

*

Eddie had kindly gone in ahead to see if the hostel had rooms, to save them dragging their cases up the steps.

'But we have booked,' the man said.

'That doesn't matter. You see, they double-book the beds. Just to ensure they fill the place. First come, first served, and, to be honest, you're a little late in the day. Let me go and check.'

Sure enough, when Eddie came bounding back down the steps, he told them they were, as he had suspected, out of luck. The couple looked concerned. 'It's not all bad news – listen, I know this place, just around the corner. You get a room to yourself, colour TV, all that. Interested? We could go and have a look.' The couple looked at each other. 'I know you're tired – and hot, and sweaty. I know I am and I haven't been carrying a case. Here, let me take that for you. Just think – in five minutes we'll have you booked in and you could have a nice shower and a Coca-Cola.'

'Is near?'

'Just round the corner,' Eddie said. 'Where you from?' Eddie asked.

'Nederlands,' the man said.

'Netherlands, eh?'

'Why you come to London?' Eddie asked.

'London?' the man said. 'Is good. Many things see. The royal family –'

'You should see them knocking about, yeah, the Queen and that.'

'And Diana – Diana fountain. We are sorry for what happen to Diana.'

'Why – it wasn't your fault, was it? Ha ha. Joke.'

'Yes, I see. And the museums.'

'Oh yeah, plenty of those – Rock Circus, Tussaud's, all dead close.'

'Natural History Museum, is close?'

'National history – it's all around you. You like Chinese food – eh? Chinks? We got Chinatown round the corner.'

'Where is the hotel?'

'Just here. That door there. Follow me.'

'You got those shackles good and attached, Killer?' Eddie asked his assistant. Killer nodded, rubbing his shaved bald head and the back of his neck which was about as thick as a tree trunk.

They had easily overpowered the couple and chained them to the bed. The bed had a gaudy bedspread. The room was unremarkable apart from the mirrored wall on one side. Eddie hadn't lied – the place was just round the corner – and the couple did have the room to themselves.

'Why you do this?' the man said, straining against the chains that held his wrists and ankles.

'You shut up,' Eddie said. 'What it is, *is*. You come to this fucking country, you play by my rules.'

'Rules?'

'Listen to me and shut up,' Eddie said. The man on the bed made as if to speak, but Eddie told him, 'You'll speak when spoken to. You got enough English to understand that?'

'Please don't hurt us. Take the money, whatever it is.'

'It's more complicated than that,' Eddie said. 'In due course I will fill you in on what it is you have to do. Don't ask me for details, because what you have to do, you will do.'

'Do?'

'Jesus, get this guy. He thinks he's on twenty fucking questions. Yes, "do". It's nothing you two haven't done before, maybe a little different from how you're used to, but Killer here will give you a little help, make sure you're doing it right. Hell, I know what people are like in hotel rooms, it'll be no different from being on holiday, so where's the harm? Anyway, we'll come to that. First things first.'

The woman stared at Eddie, slack-jawed, in shock. The man wriggled and huffed on the bed, while Killer worked the locks on the cases.

'What I want you to tell me is what you planned to do here in London. Apart from your museums and shit.'

The man looked at him blankly.

'What were you going to do? Buckingham Palace, what?' Eddie reiterated.

'Why do you want to know this?'

'Can you believe this, Killer? He answers a question with a question. Were you, or weren't you, going to go to Buckingham Palace?'

The man nodded. 'This sort of thing, yes.'

'Change of plan for you both,' Eddie said. 'How long you here for?'

'Here here?' the man said, motioning his head towards the headboard.

'Not *here*, I mean in this country.'

'One week only, then we go back.'

'OK, here's the first thing, you're going to write a postcard home, to your parents, whoever you'd send a card to, you're going to say, "London isn't so great, we decided to go to the Scottish Highlands, apparently it is beautiful up there and so on, up there in the wilderness, and we might be back a week or so later than planned." You see what I'm getting at?'

'I would not do this.'

'You won't do it – is that so? How about I *make* you do it. Or rather, Killer does.'

Killer briefly desisted from snuffling the clothes from the suitcases and throwing them all round the room, and narrowed his eyes.

'No,' the man said, 'I mean I would not send postcard. I send emails, or telephone.'

'There's no way you're doing that shit. You see an

email or telephone here? Besides, I got the cards already.'
Eddie pulled out two postcards from his jacket pocket.
One had a picture of Big Ben and 'Greetings from London'
on it. The other was a shot of Piccadilly Circus in the
1950s. He tossed them on the bed. 'Killer will undo one of
the shackles when you're ready,' Eddie said. He went
downstairs and left them to it.

Half an hour later Killer came downstairs and handed Eddie
one of the cards. Eddie slipped it in his pocket and got up.
'I'll be back later,' he said.

Eddie got out on to Shaftesbury Avenue and walked
along to Oxford Street. Jorge was in his normal place, by
the bins outside McDonald's, handing out flyers for the
Oxford English Language School. Eddie went over to him.

'Say, Jorge, will you get this translated for me?' He
handed him the postcard. 'Dutch, I think.'

'Will take about an hour. My tutor has lesson.'

'I'll be in the usual,' Eddie said.

He went across the road to the Centrepoint bar,
ordered a lime and soda, sat at a table with his drink and lit
a cigarette.

He took out his guests' wallet and purse, and a sheet of
paper, and started noting down what he could spend on
which cards, where, and when. He had to spread the
amounts, and items, logically across various times and loca-
tions. It was quite a juggling act. Priority requisitions would

require a trip across town. Some cards he could sell on. But it was no problem. This was the thin end of the wedge.

Forty minutes later Jorge appeared. He sat down and put the postcard and a piece of paper in front of Eddie. Eddie slipped him some cash. 'Don't go spending it all on nuggets, eh, Jorge,' he said.

Eddie got back to his place and went upstairs. In the room Killer was keeping an eye on the couple. He'd had to gaffer-tape the girl's mouth when for no apparent reason she'd started screaming.

'We have a problem,' Eddie said. 'I didn't post your card, Eric, and not because the post office was closed. Look at this.' The colour drained from the man Eric's face as Eddie passed the translation Jorge had given him to Killer.

It read:

Mam — please help — kidnapped — both of us — London — near hostel, west end — he try to get me to say SCOTLANDE, no, LONDON. Prisoners. PLEASE HELP. ERIC

'I don't like what you're saying there,' Eddie said. 'I'm going to leave Killer with you once more, and this time see if he can drum some sense into you. Then we'll try again.'

Eddie left the room and closed the door behind him. Halfway down the stairs he heard the man shriek.

*

The next day, Eddie was out on the street, hustling up business.

He stepped out in front of a squat, bald, middle-aged man in a baggy dark suit and sunglasses, waddling along with an air of curiosity about him.

'What are you after?' Eddie asked. 'Some action, I'd say — I can see you're a man after some action. Thing is, round here, it's all clip joints and that. They'll take your money soon as look at you. And you won't get a sniff of it.'

'What have *you* got?' the man asked, with a strong American accent.

'What I have is the real deal. Fresh meat. You'll see a young couple at it. You'll see the whole thing. You can get right up close to the action.'

'How much?'

'We can talk about that. But it's worth it. You'll be all on your own — your own cubicle, glass partition, you can do what you like. These other places, you can't do jackshit. But this — this you should see. You want to see people doing what they *shouldn't* be doing?'

The American nodded.

'And let's face it — these people don't really want to be doing what they're not supposed to be doing. But they don't have a choice, right?'

The American smiled.

'These two you're going to see,' Eddie continued. 'God's great innocents. They *really* don't want to be doing what we got them doing. You can see it in their *eyes*.'

'Is it good?' the man asked.

'Is it good?' Eddie replied. 'It's *disgusting*.'

The American thought for a moment. 'Do they . . .'

'Do they what?'

The American leaned and whispered into Eddie's ear. Eddie tapped a finger on his chin. 'Well – these two are new. But I'm sure they'll be open to suggestions. You interested?'

The American nodded.

'Then let's go.' Eddie headed off up the street. The American followed him.

'Say, what happened to your eye there?' the American asked. 'If you don't mind me asking.'

'Not at all,' Eddie said as they turned a corner. 'I'll tell you all about it.'

the islander

Roger Kingham sat at the bar, sipping his drink, wishing they'd turn down *The Best of Bob Marley*, the only tape they ever played, and wishing Red would leave him the hell alone.

'Just fifty,' Red said. 'Is all I need.'

'Red, I can't lend you the money. I'm leaving tomorrow.'

'You won't lend it to me? Me, who showed you and your buddy round the island!'

'You didn't show us round the island,' Kingham replied.

'That's it. I can show you the island *tonight*. I'll show you something like you never seen before. For the article. Up in the hills.' He made vague motions behind him, teetering on his bar stool.

'I've got everything I need for the article,' Kingham said. He'd been sent on an assignment by the magazine to the Caribbean, to do a piece on the world's oldest rum distillery. The magazine took countless thousands in advertising from the demon rum manufacturers and a piece on the drink and its history could do no harm. Kingham, believing this to be a plum assignment, was sent out with a photographer to the place in Sugar Cane Bay on the island of Tortola, in the British Virgin Islands. The photographer had got his snaps – including Kingham wearing a pith helmet and Hawaiian shirt, posing in front of the ancient stone distillery, swigging from a demijohn of the pure stuff, then headed back to Puerto Rico to fly home. Kingham had booked a few extra days to soak up some local colour for the piece. Instead, he had soaked up his bodyweight in cheap rum, caught too much sun, was scabbed with mosquito bites and felt lousy. These plum assignments always turned out to be a headache. And he'd forgotten to remind himself that he wasn't getting any younger. The trip out alone was some kind of undertaking; nine-hour flight to Miami, connection to San Juan, then a shuttle-bus ride out of San Juan to the east of the island to visit one of the new distilleries at a place called Fajardo, and a plane from there to another island, St Thomas, then a ferry ride to Tortola. All for an article that might warrant a cursory glance from the reader and a pat on the back from ad sales. At least he was leaving the next day, but his last evening in the bar was now to be plagued with Bob Marley and Red.

Red was a local, an American ex-pat drinking himself to death on a trust fund, so-named 'Red' because of his florid alcoholic mien. They'd met him on the first night at the hotel bar, and he'd seemed a nice enough fellow, but he had a problem, and his problem was that he couldn't get the booze into his system quickly enough. If he'd ever had any ambition, it was long gone, replaced with an ambition to douse every molecule in his body with alcohol. Aged twenty-eight he looked nearer forty-something, older than Kingham, and his liver surely resembled a tea bag that had been dropped, trodden on and left there. For a moment – the moment Kingham and the photographer had met him – Red had been ebullient, potentially interesting, then had hit a brick wall, started talking in tighter and tighter circles, slurring, fell off his bar stool, spilled his drinks and ordered more, became aggressive, finally staggered off and passed out. The photographer had suggested Kingham give Red a wide berth for his remaining stay, but Red had found *him*, Kingham, on his final night feeling no more adventurous than visiting the hotel bar. Red was being reasonably lucid, the plan taking shape in his head reinvigorating his depleted faculties.

'This you really should see. What do you think, Englisher?'

'What is it? Voodoo?'

'Fuck no! A crackhouse.'

'You need a fifty to visit a crackhouse?'

Red's bloodshot eyes momentarily flared. 'C'mon, man, you got magazine expenses, surely?'

'I have expenses, but I can't write off expenses as fifty dollars for our guide taking me to a crackhouse in the mountains in the dead of night. This article is about rum.'

'That's just it – I'll pay you back – I'll pay you back double, I swear.'

'Red, when will you pay me back? I'm leaving *tomorrow*.'

'Where from?'

'I get the ferry to St Thomas, then the plane to Puerto Rico.'

'That's perfect,' Red said, warming to his plan of action. 'I have to go to St Thomas tomorrow, I'll get you the money then.'

'You're going to St Thomas?'

'Every month, end of the month, the folks put my allowance in the Bank America over there. I have to go pick it up. We'll go together.'

'I have to get the ferry early.'

'No problem. Listen, I can get you on the ferry for nothing. We go to the bank – I'll show you round St Thomas.'

'I have a plane to catch.'

'What time is the plane?' Red said, looking at his watch.

'About six.'

'Plenty of time. Shit, man, St Thomas is party island. We'll have some fun then put you on your plane. I swear to God. Hey, Vincent,' Red called over to the barman. 'Ain't I going to St T tomorrow?'

'If you say so, Red,' Vincent said.

'Look, Red –' Kingham started.

'I'll get you double, I'll get you on the ferry, I'll meet you some people – I swear. Listen, come with me tonight. We'll go in the hire car.'

'I don't have a hire car. I think I'll pass anyway.'

'You gonna lend me the fifty?'

Kingham had the feeling he'd have Red at the end of his bed pleading for the money until he relented. He took out his wallet. 'This is going to leave me short.'

'Trust me, it'll be fine,' Red said.

'I have to get the early ferry. I don't want to miss my plane.'

'Me too. I want to get to the bank soon as it opens and then we're away. I'll meet you in the morning.' Red shoved the five tens into the pocket in his shorts and got down off the bar stool. 'See you then,' he said, and left in a hurry.

Kingham peered into his wallet, shook his head, then put it away. He ordered a last beer, paid his tab and said goodbye to Vincent. 'You sen' me a copy of the article,' Vincent said. 'Mek sure you mention me.'

157

'I'll send you some new CDs,' Kingham said.

He went upstairs to his room, and packed before he went to bed, and could still hear Bob Marley thudding away from the bar below.

When Kingham woke at seven, scratching his mosquito bites, it suddenly struck him – what the hell had he been thinking, lending money to Red to go and spend in a crackhouse? The barman, Vincent, had assured Kingham that yes, Red did go once a month to St Thomas to get his money. Even so, there was no way the man would meet him first thing in the morning after a night in a crackhouse. He'd be in a ditch somewhere. Besides that, they hadn't even arranged where they were going to meet. Terrific. Fifty dollars down, all to get rid of Red for the evening. He took his bag and checked out of the Sugar Cane Lodge. There was no one on the desk, so he left his key on the counter. He figured he'd stroll down to the beach and get a cab from the breakfast hut.

'Hey, Englisher,' someone called out. Sure enough, Red was sitting in the shade under a palm tree, wearing the same faded maroon Harvard University sweatshirt he'd had on the night before.

'I didn't think you'd make it somehow,' Kingham said.

Red got up. He looked pale and jittery. 'Been up all night,' he said, slapping Kingham on the arm. Kingham winced. 'I'm *still* up!'

'Shall we get a cab to the ferry?'

'No need for that. Follow me,' Red said. They set off down the hill.

Halfway down Red stopped and stepped on to the verge, knocking on the door of a corrugated shack. After a moment a door creaked open – the whites of two eyes peered out, and a bony hand proffered two brown bottles with red-and-white labels and the tops off. Red took them and got back on the road. He offered one of the bottles to Kingham.

'Too early for me,' Kingham said.

'Never too early,' Red said, and took a long gulp of beer, foam running down his chin, the red flooding back into his skin.

At the bottom of the hill, as if on cue, a white pickup with tinted windows came tearing round the corner and screeched to a halt as Red waved it down. The driver's window came down. A dude with black wraparounds and a goatee looked at them.

'Take us to the ferry?' Red said, before draining the bottle and tossing it.

The driver thumbed them to get in the back. They had barely climbed in when the pickup careened down the hill at high speed, taking a tight corner and throwing Red and Kingham around in the back like two pensioners on the *Titanic*, Kingham clutching on to his bag and the side of the truck for dear life, Red holding his second bottle of beer to his chest like a crucifix.

A mile or so later the pickup stopped at a T-junction. The driver signalled them to get out. They had barely touched the tarmac when it had torn off down the road.

'It's only a mile down here,' Red said, pointing the other way, and they began to walk. Kingham could see some buildings, the blue, blue sea in the distance. It was hotting up now, and on they walked, Red sucking down his beer, chattering incessantly about the delights of St Thomas. 'I'll take you to Mango's bar. That place hits it. You'll love it. There are some girls I know there. Wooo-eee. See, it's an American colony – all-American, and we know how to do it! Party town. Not like those lazy fucks back there sat around in do-nothingsville all day. St T is the place. With some money in our pocket, we'll have a party before you go home. You won't want to leave!'

'Why don't you live there?' Kingham asked. Red shrugged, finished the beer and his eyes started to dart around ferociously like a coyote looking for a rabbit. He pointed to a low white stucco building standing alone about two hundred yards away.

'We'll get a drink in there before we get the ferry.'

'Shouldn't we get to the terminal first?'

'They won't go without us.'

Kingham was anxious – the sort of nervous anxiety you get when you have connections to make and any sort of detour might buck the scheme of things. He just wanted to get to St Thomas, get his money and make sure he got his plane. But Red was already picking his way through a tattered chicken-wire fence and making for the white building. Kingham followed. There was some time before the ferry.

Red knocked on the door of the building.

'They open?' Kingham asked.

'Soon will be.'

There was the sound of locks being drawn back and bolts unbolted and the door swung open. A man in a vest with a black beard stood there.

'OK for a drink, Jay?' Red asked.

Jay tipped his head to signal them in.

At least it was nice and cool in there, Kingham thought. He'd worked up a terrible sweat even though they'd walked only half a mile and he was toting just a holdall.

They took down two stools from the long wooden bar and sat there. Jay set up two beers, and by now Kingham was in the mood for one.

'Good, huh?' Red said, froth sitting like a moustache on his upper lip.

Kingham felt himself relax a little. Why not? He had his story, he was on his way home, and he was going to get an extra fifty dollars and a free ferry ride into the bargain. That wasn't so bad.

They finished their beers and, as seemed to be the manner of things, Red led on the expedition. 'Thanks, Jay. I'll settle when I get back from St T with some doh-ray-me.'

Jay nodded, which reassured Kingham that Red was as good as his word. He'd turned up on time and the bar owner was prepared to trust him.

There was quite a crowd at the ferry terminal office queuing to get tickets. The ferry left in fifteen minutes. Red pulled Kingham to one side away from the queue. He approached two ferry officials in blue shirts with name tags.

Red addressed one of them, a fat, stern-looking black woman. 'Selena, I want to get my friend here on the ferry.'

'Then he can get in that queue and buy himself a ticket.'

'I told him I —'

'I don't care what you told him. We let you on because we have an arrangement, but he has to buy a ticket.'

'It's OK,' Kingham said, reaching for his wallet.

'Now hold on,' Red said to Selena, who was glaring at him. 'I said I'd get him on the ferry and I'm going to get him on the ferry.'

'Then *you* buy his ticket.'

Red ran his hand through his hair. 'Don't give me this shit —'

Selena pointed a finger at him. 'Don't *you* give me any shit, Red, or *you* won't get on that ferry.'

Kingham got in the queue. 'I'll see you on board,' Red told him. 'I'll be in the bar.'

No shit, Kingham thought, as he stood in the queue, about half a dozen people in front of him.

*

The ride across from Tortola to St Thomas on the small ferry was quite choppy, but mercifully short. Kingham decided to stand on the top deck rather than prop up the bar with Red, who was drinking down plastic beakers of Red Stripe at some pace. The guy would be dead soon, Kingham considered. He had pieced together that Red was in some kind of enforced exile, sent about as far away from his folks on the mainland as was possible, to a small island where he could be little nuisance to the family and drink the local rum at two dollars a bottle. He seemed like an intelligent enough guy, but the booze had him in a stranglehold, he was in thrall to it, and nothing was going to end that doomed romance. God knows, Kingham liked a drink himself, but this guy made him feel like the President of the Temperance Society. He breathed in the sea air and felt the breeze soothe his itching bites, and his heart lifted as St Thomas came into view.

As they docked, Kingham went down to the bar to find Red. The shutter was closed and Red was nowhere to be seen. He went down the gangway and got into another queue filing through passport control, craning to see Red ahead of him in the queue. But he couldn't and guessed he would meet him on the other side. The anxiety came back – typical at any checkpoint, particularly one with a big sign reading 'YOU ARE NOW ENTERING THE UNITED STATES OF AMERICA'; not improved by what appeared to be a tussle at the head of the queue, two officials with pistols on their belts moving in to deal with some small commotion. The sooner Kingham showed his passport the better.

Once through, Kingham found himself pretty much straight out on to the street. It was blazing hot. He put on his sunglasses and fanned himself with his passport. Red was nowhere to be seen. Shit, had that guy given him the jump? Surely not. Why bother meeting up with him at all if he was going to do that? He waited some more, slowly sweating. Still plenty of time before his plane.

Red didn't show. Kingham went back into the ferry terminal. It had emptied out. He checked the men's toilets and called out Red's name. Nothing. He thought of asking someone, but thought better of it. The officials gave you such steely glances that you felt just asking them the time might end up with you in a room with no windows.

Kingham figured it out. Red had probably gone straight to the bank, probably too boozed and dazed to remember he had a travelling companion, just thinking of the 'doh-ray-me', and more sauce.

The main drag of St Thomas – which was all it amounted to – a long straight strip carved down the middle of the island – started left out of the terminal. A gruesome parade of shops and restaurants and more shops, all with tropical themes, lone palm trees and tourists in white logoed T-shirts and baseball hats with parrots on, sucking on Popsicles or draining down chug-alug sodas from big styrofoam cups, under the blue, blue sky.

Kingham was dizzy with walking by the time he'd found the Bank America, tucked away in one of the mini-malls — fountains and potted palms and racks and racks of shit for sale — thankful for the air conditioning as he went in. There was nobody queuing, so he weaved around the snaking rope barrier and stanchions and up to a window.

'I wonder if you can help. I'm looking for a friend. He was supposed to come here this morning.' That was one advantage the English had, Kingham thought. The Americans loved a Brit accent. Their eyes would light up and they'd say, 'Where you from?' It was an in.

'Huh?'

'A friend — I'm meeting him — he's supposed —'

'You're meeting a friend in a bank.'

'There's been some confusion.'

'You have an account here?'

'No. I just wanted to know if he'd been in here.'

'Does he have an account here?'

'Oh, yes.'

'I'm afraid client information is confidential, sir.'

'I don't want any information — just whether he's been in, he's about this tall, red-faced —'

'What's his name?'

'Red.'

'Red what?'

'Red what?'

'What's his full name?'

'Shit. I only know him as Red.'

'Sir, I'd prefer it if you'd refrain from using profanities.'

'I'm sorry. I mean – I really need to –'

'Would you like me to get the manager?'

This sounded to Kingham more like a threat than an offer of assistance. 'No, it's OK, thank you,' he said, making his way to the door and knocking over one of the stanchions on the way out.

He sat on the edge of the fountain and considered his options. He could hoick up and down the horror of the St Thomas main drag looking for Red and his money, or give it up as a lost cause and make his way to the airport and just get the hell out of there. He devised a compromise. He'd ring the airport, find out the check-in time, and then spend a few hours mooching around on the off chance. From what he'd seen of the 'airport' – a half-finished breeze-block building with a short landing strip, and a vending machine for refreshments – it was not the sort of place he'd want to spend more time than he had to.

Walking back along the main drag, the sidewalks were brimming, and Kingham ducked into a car park where a phone booth stood alone in the middle of the cracked concrete lot.

He fed some coins into the phone and, cradling the

receiver in the crook of his neck, wrestled his plane ticket out of the outside zip pocket of his holdall. Someone prodded him in the ribs.

He turned to see a greasy little geek looking up at him. 'Hey, Mac, spare me some change?'

'Sorry – I just put my money in the phone here.'

The small man became aggressive very quickly, hustling him into the booth, prodding him and saying, 'You fuck, you fucking tourists come over here, you fuck us all over –'

Kingham pushed him away. 'Hey – I'm trying to make a call. I didn't do anything.'

'Ach,' the man said in disgust, and walked away.

Kingham recomposed himself and rang the airport. At least he tried to. He could never get the hang of the American phone system. You had to talk to an operator and choose a phone company and get connected and feed in more dimes and even then no one answered. Little wonder considering that two-bit airport. The pilot probably answered the phone and refilled the vending machine. God, how he wished he'd gone back with the photographer.

Kingham hung up the phone. His plan was simple – he'd find a bar, have a drink, cool off. The incident with that little punk had left him flustered and the fact that his good pal Red had burned him was upsetting, so a few drinks would take the edge off things, and be some help in braving the short but terrifying flight in the eight-seater prop that would take him to Puerto Rico. He wasn't especially scared of flying, but anyone would be in a biscuit tin with shuddering wings. Best not think about it.

Then it hit him. *Mango's bar*. That's where treacherous Red would be. Kingham, encouraged, grabbed his holdall and made his way back to the main drag.

It wasn't hard to find the place – it had a big yellow sign and heavy wood-panelled doors. Kingham went in. It was devoid of customers, but Kingham's disappointment was offset by the relief of getting away from that glorified outdoor tropical shopping mall, the feverish guzzling and squawking and sweating of that fat moronic crowd. He sat up at the bar and ordered a beer from the tanned, muscled barman wearing a T-shirt that said 'Life's a bitch and then you marry one'.

The beer propped in front of him, Kingham took a napkin and wrote out his itinerary. The plane was at seven. He should get to the airport at six. Give himself half an hour to get *there*. It was now twelve thirty. He had an age. Funny that he'd felt the need to get the early ferry, just to be sure, always to be sure. There were only two ferries a day, and he could have taken the afternoon boat, but that would have been cutting it fine, and what if it had been delayed, cancelled? No point hanging around. Pack your bag and go.

After a couple of beers he relaxed and ordered a burger. It came with fries and a sliver of gherkin on a platter. He didn't realise how hungry and thirsty he'd become traipsing around all day without so much as a knotted hankerchief on his head.

'You gonna be guzzling beer,' the barman said, 'might as well take a pitcher. Works out cheaper in the long run.'

What the heck, Kingham thought. He could put that on expenses. 'Refreshments.' 'Beverages', whatever. Might as well get a load on for that dreaded flight. What the hell! He didn't feel so bad. He needn't tell anyone about the Red business. Put it down to experience. He poured himself a tall glass.

Kingham had done three-quarters of the pitcher of Bud when the door of the bar swung open. A figure was silhouetted against the light.

Red? Kingham thought. The man came down the steps to the bar floor, teetering ever so slightly. It wasn't Red.

'Out,' the barman snapped.

The man looked at him dizzily, turned, and went out.

'Don't like to upset our customers,' the barman said to Kingham. Kingham nodded, and took another slurp of beer.

'Mind if I throw on some music?' the barman asked.

'No problemo,' Kingham said.

'No Woman, No Cry' sounded from the speakers. Kingham cringed. Party town my arse, he thought. As for this crowd of women. Red was a real bastard. Kingham finished off his pitcher and asked for the bill.

The barman totted it up and slipped it in front of him. Oops! Forty-two dollars for 'refreshments'. Ah well, fuck 'em, they sell enough magazines.

He reached for his wallet, reached for it and didn't find it. He panic-pattered his pockets, and it was not there. In his bag perhaps? He hurriedly unzipped the side pocket, the top zip. Nothing. Oh no – the weasel at the phone booth. He'd been stung. Stung and stung again! All his cash and his credit cards. Good God! Ten dollars and change in his back pocket did not a forty-dollar bill plus tips make.

'Something the matter, buddy?' the barman said.

'My wallet – stolen –'

The barman didn't say anything.

'Outside at the – I – this guy – shit – I –'

The barman nodded. 'No money. You come in here and drink your fill and eat yourself a Mango-burger but neglect the fact you have no money.'

'I had a – look – I –' Kingham reached into his bag and pulled out a copy of the magazine. 'I'm a writer – I – the magazine will – I can give you the name of –'

The barman took the magazine. 'Beer and a meal in exchange for a magazine,' he said. 'Good deal, considering it ain't even a titty magazine.'

'There are some tits in there,' Kingham pleaded.

'Yeah, but no PUSSY!' the barman said, tearing the magazine in two and throwing it to the floor.

'It's OK,' Kingham said. 'Really – this guy Red – he's

– I'm meeting him here. He owes me a hundred.'

'You know Red?'

'Certainly. He's a friend of mine. He's coming here to meet me with the money.'

The barman nodded, coming round the bar. 'Any friend of Red is a friend of mine.'

The barman stood over Kingham. Kingham frowned. The barman cracked Kingham in the face and sent him reeling off his bar stool.

'That fucking punk owes me several fucking thousand in lost profits. Damn near lost me my licence.'

On the floor, Kingham felt a welter of blows as the barman leaned into him. He then picked him up by his hair, and threw him out on to the street. Kingham's holdall followed shortly afterwards, hitting him on the head.

Kingham dragged himself up in front of a crowd of staring tourists, good people, good people he was sure, and scurried away, weeping.

'The airport please,' Kingham said.

The cab driver shook his head.

'Please, I need to get to the airport.' He waved the scrunched-up ten-dollar bill.

'No, sir, no like that.'

Kingham caught his reflection in the back window of the cab. His face swelling up fast, blood all down his shirt.

'How far is the airport?' Kingham sobbed.

The driver pointed.

Kingham started walking.

It was a two-mile walk. Kingham went into a makeshift men's room and washed his face and changed into a clean T-shirt. He was in a state of shock. He barely registered getting on to the plane, the Sellotape and staples holding the wings together, the pilot who looked like he was about to have a heart attack, the dreadful rattling of the propellers, none of it. He was in a horrible daze, and when the plane landed and bounced around on the runway his head hurt and his body hurt and his wallet was gone and he walked out of the airport and into the small town, half a mile to the town square, where the sun was going down and men were playing draughts outside the bars and the locals wandered aimlessly around. Kingham stood at the bus stop with his holdall, occasionally shaking his head to bring himself to, and then the sun had gone down and it became apparent that he had missed the last shuttle out of there.

He asked some of the men outside the bars how he might get to San Juan, but his Spanish was as bad as their English. They shrugged, he gestured, a taxi driver laughed at his ten dollars — he had had it with taxi drivers — and he wandered away from the town square, feeling like the guy at the end of *Midnight Cowboy*, all of a sudden very alone.

*

Somewhere on the outskirts of the town, to the left of the road, was a sandbank; beyond it, in the black, the sound of the ocean. Kingham resolved to go and sleep on the beach. At least the sand would be soft. But the thought of it appalled him – he was too old for this wearying nonsense. As he climbed the sandbank he turned, hearing something. Across the road, rising above the single-storey houses around it, was an old-style Spanish church. He would throw himself at the mercy of the sweet Lord Jesus! He slid down the sandbank and across the road to the church, crept into one of the pews at the back, and sat listening to the sermon in Spanish. Elderly men and women, children, a sizeable congregation, sat with their heads bowed. Kingham's head was bowed too, but for a different reason.

When he woke, there was a crowd around him; they were looking at him like he was the Second Coming, chattering in Spanish, which he didn't understand. He sat up straight and tried to explain his predicament. Nobody understood a thing, but many crossed themselves. *No hablo español*, he told them, and tried, with aching limbs, to mime his situation. One of them, surely, would take him in and feed him soup for the night. But they looked confused and bewildered. It was a stalemate and the congregation began to file out, back to their homes, their beds, their *things*. An old man with a grey moustache and kind eyes stayed. Kingham pointed. 'I sleep – on the beach – *la playa* –' He made as if to sleep, both hands resting at the side of his head. The old man wagged a finger vigorously. Then he pointed in the direction of the ocean, and slowly drew his hand across his throat. Kingham understood that if he slept on the beach, his throat would surely be cut. Kingham left with the old man and they went their separate ways.

He made his way back into the town. The town square was dark now. There was no one around. Not a soul, not even a cat. He kept walking. He was in the full grip of despair now – pained, tired, hungry, thirsty, all but broke, nowhere to sleep, no hope in sight. He tried to think of a happy place, which, perversely enough, would normally have been a tropical island with sandy beaches and swaying palms. Right now it was the dismal one-bedroom flat a journalist's wages could cover in North Kilburn.

He saw a blue light ahead. It would pain him if it turned out to be a sign for a motel bearing a Visa logo. He'd passed two of those already. As he drew closer he could make it out. It read 'POLICIA'.

'Abla anglaise?' he asked the night-shift cop behind the tiny desk in the world's smallest police station.

'A little.'

Kingham told his tale.

The cop shrugged. They did a lot of shrugging in this part of the world, Kingham noticed.

'What I'm saying is, I need somewhere to sleep.'

'We have nowhere.'

Kingham paused, then said. 'How about I sleep in a cell?'

'We only have one cell.'

'Anyone in it?'

'Wha?'

'The cell – is it *ocupado*?'

'No.'

'Could I sleep in it?'

'We need cell – in case we bring someone in.'

'Who are you going to bring in?' Apart from the guy, it struck him, who slit throats on the beach.

The cop shrugged again.

'Let me sleep in there. If you need it, you can wake me up.'

The cop shook his head. Kingham considered getting himself arrested, but felt that an unprovoked attack on a policeman wouldn't get him home any quicker, and a confession to being the beach throat slitter would never be taken seriously.

'You can sleep on the bench.' He pointed down the corridor to a narrow wooden bench against the wall.

Kingham shrugged himself, for the hell of it, and went and lay down.

The chances of sleep were zero. It wasn't the fluorescent lights, the thinness and hardness of the bench, the lack of a quilt. It was the noticeboard on the wall opposite, festooned with what looked like the cast of America's Most Wanted. Puerto Rico was a common jumping-off point for felons. They could get down there easily enough, it was part of the US. And there were a million islands and a thousand crude ways of getting to them from there. The noticeboard was hanging off the wall under the weight of dozens and dozens of photostats of criminal rap sheets, which Kingham could not stop himself from reading. Murderers, arsonists, armed robbers, rapists, perverts, coke dealers, dope smugglers, kidnappers, gang bangers, more killers, gunrunners, all leered down at him, their mugshots distorted on the crude black-and-white printouts. There was no doubt about it, these were ugly fellows with evil faces, not a Ted Bundy among them, and they were all staring down at their new companion. John 'Chipmunk' Benson, the child-strangler, with his buck-teeth and weasly beard, seemed to take a particularly keen interest in Kingham. Kingham turned over to face the wall but could feel Chipmunk's eyes boring into the back of his head, and hear Chipmunk's voice saying, 'Don't worry, pal, I don't care if you ain't a kid, I'll kill ya just the same, I'll ask you ya three favourite colours then I'll strangle ya!' Kingham couldn't stand it. He got up, grabbed his holdhall and fled the safety of the police station.

He walked, and walked, and thought, if I keep walking the sun will come up and a bus will come and this nightmare will be over. He walked up a hill and the houses thinned out and he saw a half-built place off to one side of the road. He went in and saw it had a roof and saw there was a roll of old carpet. It would do, it would have to do. He fashioned a bed out of some discarded planks and laid down the carpet and put his holdall down as a pillow, and thought, all for an article on rum.

Just then his heart sang. With something approaching elation he unzipped the holdall and reached into the bottom, and felt it there, the smooth, cool, glass curves. He pulled out a small bottle of the good stuff, a gift from the distillery. He pulled out the cork and took a long, long swallow. The fire burned in him, he rolled his shoulders and thought, tonight I will sleep and tomorrow all will be well. Then he took another drink.

Chipmunk, the buck-toothed killer, came and stood over Kingham in the darkness. He prodded him once in the neck with his knife, then again, until Kingham rolled over and looked up at him. Kingham was confused. What was with the knife – didn't Chipmunk strangle his victims? Kingham watched in terror as the killer leaned in and plunged the short blade into his neck. He woke with a scream, a black cat flying through the air. He scrambled out of his makeshift bed, dusting himself down, and shuddered. He took his bag, and picked his way out, leaving behind him a small empty glass bottle and a discarded cork. The cat stood there with its fur bristling, watching him go.

I'll probably get arrested now, Kingham thought, for trespass, and vagrancy. He walked down to the town square and waited for the first bus to arrive. He'd never felt so tired. The rum had knocked him out but was still working him over. One night had put three years on him.

The bus pulled up, Kingham got on and went to the back and slept all the way to San Juan.

Red had been hustled out of the queue at the ferry terminal by two guards with pistols on their belts and taken into a room with no windows.

'Monthly visit, eh, Red?' the man in a shirt and epaulettes said.

'Yeah, I always come this time,' Red said.

'And you're supposed to ring and arrange.'

'Ah, come on.'

'Come on nothing. You know the deal.'

'I won't cause any trouble.'

'You don't cause trouble, Red, you *are* trouble.'

'I'm OK.'

'Red, we got a call from Tortola – Selena said you were already causing shit before you got on the ferry.'

'That was just a mix-up.'

'Well, there's no mix-up now. You're gonna sit here –'

'I need to get to the bank.'

'I understand that – what I don't understand is why they can't wire the money across. Anyway. You're gonna sit here and wait until Rudy gets back and he will escort you to the bank to pick up your money and escort you back here and you'll sit and wait until the afternoon ferry takes you back home. OK?'

'I can get to the bank and back on my own.'

'Red, you are bad for business. St Thomas does not like things that are bad for business.'

'Shit, there's worse'n me out there.'

'But you're not out there, Red, which is a start. We'll wait for Rudy.'

'I wanted to show my friend from England a good time on the island.'

'I'm sure he'll have plenty of fun with or without you.'

'Sure,' Red said, leaning back in defeat. 'It's a fun place. Say, could I get a drink?'

A couple of months later, Red walked into the bar at the Sugar Cane Lodge and asked Vincent for an early-morning beer.

Vincent set up the beer and said, 'Today I got sent a copy of that magazine they wrote about us.'

'You did?' Red said.

'The guy he say I'm the best barman on the island. Gonna frame it and hang it right here behind the bar! There

was a note in there – the guy say, 'If you see Red tell him
he owes me one hundred dollars.'

'What guy?'

'The Englishman.'

Red narrowed his eyes and looked at Vincent, and said,
'What Englishman?' and meant it.

orson beadle, cinema manager

A small ad in the back of the paper read:

Picture House
Now Showing
Night of the Succubus
Final night Friday, 7pm.
See what everyone's been talking about.
Not just a film, an 'experience'!
In 'MONDOVISION'

Times weren't good for cinema trade, but Orson Beadle was never one to let the public mood get in the way of him selling them things they didn't need; in this case, a cinema ticket. Beadle's small, one-screen cinema was playing a crude horror film, which was doing good business in spite of its crudity, and thanks to Beadle's own newly patented 'MONDOVISION'. The cinema building itself, a pizza place to one side, a hairdresser on the other, wasn't much: white plaster, wooden frames to hold the posters, illuminated with lamps, corniced double doors and a purple-carpeted lobby that became crowded mercifully quickly. A combination ticket booth/concession stand set to the left-hand side sold bags of popcorn, ice creams and sweets. The auditorium was cavernous, ill-ventilated, with a slight rake and the rows of seats set too closely together. The curtains parted in the middle and were supposed to slide back smoothly, but the mechanism was rickety and made an excessive amount of noise. The sound system was decrepit – two large speakers choked with dust sat on the stage behind the moth-eaten cinema screen. Ordinarily these shortcomings might cause a manager concern, but Beadle wasn't worried. After all, he had MONDOVISION.

At half past six, Beadle descended the stairs from the office-cum-projection booth to get things ready for the evening's performance. He was inspecting the carpet for crumbs when he heard a strange sucking noise from behind the concession stand.

'Monteith – is that you, Monteith?' Beadle called out.

Monteith's head popped up from behind the stand. He was chewing furiously, mustard running down his chin.

Monteith was Beadle's assistant, a very short, humpbacked man with a club foot and a face like a walnut.

'What on earth are you doing?' Beadle asked.

Monteith swallowed, then spoke. 'Just seeing the hot dogs are OK.'

'And are they?'

Monteith nodded. 'Delicious.'

'Well, don't test all of them,' Beadle said, walking across the lobby. 'That's our profit margin you're eating.'

Beadle noted, as he opened the cinema doors to let the customers in, that a decent-sized queue had formed outside – young and old, families and couples, a good, mixed crowd. Word must have spread about MONDOVISION, Beadle thought, and the newspaper ad can't have hurt either. There were even a few faces he'd see at previous showings, he was sure of that, coming back for more – no better recommendation. Why sell someone something once, when you can sell them something twice, or even three times? That was Beadle's philosophy.

Beadle sold the tickets and sweets, while Monteith stood two yards away, by the doors to the auditorium, tearing the tickets and getting each and every customer to sign a form that exempted the management from liability for *anything* that might befall said customer during the screening. The patrons thought this was a wonderful hoot, and filed in in curious anticipation, sitting on the creaky fold-down chairs with their bags of sweets and hot dogs and choc ices and cups of cola, quite unaware that they'd just signed a fully binding legal document. Beadle couldn't take any risks with MONDOVISION – you never knew how people might react. As Beadle well knew, you can please most of the people, most of the time, but you can upset a good proportion of them pretty easily too. You had to keep these things at the forefront of one's mind when running a business, Beadle knew only too well.

Monteith tore the last ticket then sped up the stairs to the projection booth to start the film.

A young, eager-looking man, clutching a notepad, came in as Beadle was closing up the stand.

'Am I too late?' the man said.

'Just on time,' Beadle told him.

'I'm reviewing this for the local paper,' the man said. 'It's my first assignment. They said they might make me their regular film reviewer.'

'Well, in you go,' Beadle said. 'This is on me. Good luck to you.'

'Could I get a quote from you, for the article?'

'Certainly,' Beadle said. 'Regarding?'

'Just something about what you offer, that other cinemas don't.'

'Of course, of course.' Beadle thought for a moment, rearranging the bags of Fruit Pastilles. 'These are testing times for cinema owners,' Beadle started. 'With home entertainment taking great strides forward, people can get cinema-quality sound in their own homes on screens nearly as big as cinema screens, enjoy crisp pictures, in focus – even we can't offer *that*! People want more – they always want more – and someone has to provide that, or they won't be satisfied. They'll turn their backs. The point I'm making here is that the cinema has to compete, as they did in the fifties when television first threatened –'

'With 3-D you mean?' the man asked, as he scribbled away on his notepad.

'Exactly,' Beadle said, 'giving away 3-D glasses, they tried all sorts. But those were just gimmicks. MONDOVISION is no gimmick.'

'What exactly *is* "MONDOVISION"?'

'We've pulled out all the stops with MONDOVISION – so you really *experience* the film. The cinema itself might be a bit run down, and the *films* are certainly dilapidated, but in MONDOVISION you'll get a night's entertainment you'll never forget!'

'But what *exactly* –?'

'Step right in, and you'll see. You'd better hurry! Here, have one of these for the film –'

He pushed a choc ice into the journalist's hand, ushered him into the auditorium and closed the doors.

The film began. It was a scratched, cracked print, but the audience paid that no heed, for almost as soon as it had started the footage of car crashes and open-heart surgery, culled from public information films and carefully spliced into the first reel by Monteith, began appearing on-screen; pretty soon the audience had lost any thread of the narrative of *Night of the Succubus*, distracted as they were by Monteith's gut-wrenching inserts – indeed, one old lady was sick into her bag, and made a big commotion of it, and several couples got up to leave. They were unable to get a refund as Beadle was in his office counting the evening's takings.

The old lady staggered out of the auditorium after them, wiping her mouth, then tore off her wig and jacket and dashed up the stairs into the projection booth.

'The switch, Monteith, throw the switch!' Beadle called out from behind his piles of coins, as he saw Monteith come in. Just in time, Monteith cranked the lever that ran the second reel, then hurriedly changed into his next costume. Moments later he ran down the aisle, wearing a ghoul mask, black top and trousers, brandishing a rubber carving knife. He hauled a young woman from her seat and pretended to savage her, scattering her popcorn everywhere. He let the woman collapse in a heap in the aisle, then leaped on to the stage and did a strange Egyptian-style dance, blocking half the screen. Nothing of this had anything to do with what was unfolding on-screen, but much of the audience whooped and cheered and threw popcorn none the less. Monteith went to the side of the screen and pulled out the fire hose, which he turned on, dousing the audience from rows A to Z. Some of the seats collapsed as the patrons rocked back in a vain attempt to avoid the jets of water. Next, Monteith dropped the fire hose and went behind the screen, where he released two pulleys, lowering a pair of burning papier-mâché skulls which immediately set fire to the curtains. He then charged back up to the projection booth to start the next reel.

He passed Beadle coming down the steps.

'What do you think, boss?' Monteith asked.

'More Mondo, Monteith,' Beadle said.

'More Mondo?'

Beadle nodded.

As Beadle stepped into the lobby, a pale-looking man came out of the auditorium.

'Disgusting! Revolting – VILE!' he stammered.

'Isn't it?' Beadle said. 'Just wait 'til you see the ending.'

'Not the FILM! This *hot dog*.' The man held out a withered weiner. 'I think I found a TOENAIL in it!'

'Keep your voice down,' Beadle said, 'everyone will want one.'

The man shook his head. 'Let me have some of those toffee chews.' Beadle handed him a packet and the man went back in.

The third reel opened with a warning card that filled the entire screen: 'WHAT YOU ARE ABOUT TO SEE ACTUALLY HAPPENED.' There followed a fifteen-minute sequence of a Labrador giving birth to pups. The audience wailed and moaned through the whole thing – one man had a turn, falling off his chair into the aisle with his trousers round his ankles – but after all this excitement they had worked up quite an appetite, so that by the time the intermission came round, they had quite forgotten the butchered version of *Night of the Succubus* and formed a rowdy queue to buy more sweets, and ices, from Monteith, now dressed as an usherette, carrying a lighted tray at the front of the auditorium. More mayhem followed in the second half – Monteith ran amok, clambering over seats and molesting the audience, tearing at their clothes and making obscene noises. When the film burned up in the gate, the audience bayed for blood, and Monteith had to play them a cartoon to placate them, while he fixed the film with Sellotape; later on, a fake title card was projected informing the audience that rioting had broken out in the town and that everyone would have to be locked in the cinema for the night. The climax of *Night of the Succubus* was intercut with footage of the 1972 Munich Olympics, and Monteith discharged several fireworks through the projector hatch. Someone's hair caught light but was quickly doused with the contents of a cola cup.

The credits had rolled and the lights had come on, and the audience had made their weary way to the exit doors. The last patron, the reviewer for the local paper, covered in ice cream, both the sleeves of his jacket torn off, sat there among the chaos – the broken seats and sodden carpet and smouldering skull heads – finishing his notes. It was rather fun, he'd thought – he could quite get used to this – a free ticket, and a choc ice – and he'd surely give it a very enthusiastic write-up. He had enjoyed the innovative cutting, the interaction, and particularly the old-fashioned touch of having an usherette; he had to reach way back into his childhood to remember anything like that. And, after all, wasn't that what the movies were all about – recapturing childhood? That lost innocence. It reminded him of when he was a kid and he had gone to see *Raiders of the Lost Ark* – it had been so thrilling, he'd nearly jumped in the air. After the film had finished he'd left the cinema, turned on his heel and gone straight back in for the next show. When the hero was hanging off the bottom of the truck, you felt as though you were too. Cinema was all about you being part of the experience. MONDOVISION certainly took care of that! They were on to something here, he thought. He hadn't been able to make much sense of the film, but who cared – most plots were garbage these days anyway – this was more about the imagery, the 'happening'. Yes, they were most definitely on to some-thing. As he scribbled away, he felt something brush against his ankle. He looked down, and screamed, as something sharp bit through his sock.

*

Outside in the lobby, Beadle was tacking up a poster for the next engagement, a film called *Killsquad*. 'Mind if I finish these off, boss?' Monteith asked, pointing at the hot dogs.

'Be my guest, be my guest,' Beadle said, smoothing out the creases on the poster.

Just then, the doors to the auditorium burst open, and the reviewer came barrelling out, flailing his leg and screaming, pieces of notepaper whirling up all around him.

'How did you enjoy the film?' Beadle asked. 'I trust we'll get a good review?'

'The rats,' the man cried out. 'The rats!' He charged out on to the street.

Beadle frowned, puzzled. 'Rats? What do you know about rats, Monteith?'

'Rats?' Monteith said, chomping on a hot dog. 'Don't know anything about no rats.' He swallowed and reached for another.

mitch

I did not mean to kill that man. It was an accident, sometimes I don't know my own strength, but the fact is I *did* kill him and my lawyer says there's not much he can do about *that*. While I am waiting to stand trial they've put me in with all the other murderers and killers and man-slaughterers, even though we have not been found guilty yet (but my lawyer says I probably will be found guilty on account of my colour, so it doesn't make much difference). This one fellow I'm sitting next to in the mess hall, he says, 'What you in for?' And I tell him what happened, that I didn't mean to do it; well, he killed his wife and best friend 'in cold blood', and he says to me, 'Nigger, what makes you any different? Whether you killed a man, a woman, a child, you still *killed* them.' I told him it was an accident, and he just laughed and said, 'Hell, being born was an accident for most people if you ask me.'

My wife and boys did visit but I told them not to, she said why? and I said, just don't, write to me instead and I'll write back. My wife said she is trying to raise my bail but I said no, it's too much, you got little enough as it is, the state don't pay enough to feed a chicken and you got three strong boys to take care of.

My lawyer visited me today and told me to expect a special visitor, he didn't tell me who but just said, 'Listen to what the man has to say, you might find it interesting,' and I said, 'What is it about?' He said, 'I won't talk about it now.' I said, 'Is it about getting me free?' and he said it was, in a manner of speaking.

I'd forgotten all about it until one of the guards said there was someone to see me, and I couldn't think who it might be; it wouldn't be my wife and kids, I'd told them not to come and they didn't, and my lawyer only comes once a week, if at all, he's awful busy, so I go through and a man in a suit introduces himself as a colleague of my lawyer and says he has a proposal for me. He says from what he understands I may just get away with manslaughter for what I did, and I said, yes it was an accident, but he says, taking into account what I did when I was younger (I don't do that no more, I have a wife and kids to support now), and that the facts of the matter are not clear-cut, I may get put in prison for premedicated murder, which might not be the chair, but it *will* be life, that much is certain. He said it won't be too nice for my family if I'm locked away all that time and I couldn't disagree with him. He says how are they going to survive without me to take care of them, what will your wife do? – and I'd been thinking the very same thing, that had been causing me many sleepless nights, apart from the noise from the other cells; she needs a man around, so what if she took up with another man while I'm stuck inside? – she might just have to, state benefit's worth shit – I couldn't stand the thought of her taking up with another man, or another man raising his hand to my boys if they got out of line which they're bound to do, they're just growing boys, it's bound to happen; or worse than that, what if she went back to doing what she was doing when I met her, she might have to do that too, just to raise some money, just to look after the boys; I couldn't bear that, that would tear me apart being stuck in *here* knowing she was doing that and not being able to do anything about it. That was what the fight was about, you see, one of her people, like a ghost from the past, making trouble, I was only trying to get him the hell away from her, and look what that got me. And what if my boys fall into bad ways the way I did, with no one to guide them? I swore I wouldn't let it happen the way it did to me, and that's exactly what's happening. But anyway, this friend of the lawyer, he says he has an option, that *I* might like to consider, whereby I get out of prison and my family get taken care of so they don't have to consider those *other* options. I said, well, I would certainly be interested in hearing all about it. He opened his briefcase and took out a folder and said, 'Mr Mitchell, I'd like to tell you about the process.'

It didn't take me too long to make my mind up and sign the forms. After all, what was going to happen to me? I might go to the chair anyway. Either that or be locked up in here for the rest of time. At least this way my family was taken care of (*well* taken care of, they said), and I don't get to rot in jail. The company they pay my bail, which seemed pretty high to me, but the company man he told me, 'Our clients are happy to pay a very good price for someone like you.' I got to visit my family one more time before they took me in. It was terrible and sad to leave them like that, but it's what would have happened anyway.

The place is pretty nice, and even though we are not allowed out it's not like prison – there's good food, I don't have to share my room – that's the difference – it's a room, not a cell. I still miss my wife and the boys, but I met some people, we become friends. This one guy, he's a funny old guy, he plays chess with himself (he's not in here for the same thing, a lot of them aren't, I don't tell them what I did), he keeps ribbing me, saying, 'You'll go quickly,

Mitchell, very quickly, they'll *love* you!' and I don't mind about that, maybe sooner'll be better and just get it all over with. He wanted to teach me to play chess but I said, what's the point?

We've got a screening this afternoon where they choose people, I don't care if it's me, just as long as my wife and boys are OK I'm prepared. Be a shame to leave here though. Life never treated me too well, but they've treated me real nice in here. Real nice.

Also available from Vintage

DAVID L. HAYLES

The Suicide Kit

'Beautifully drawn characters...Hayles writes with such cold-blooded precision'
Guardian

David L. Hayles's debut collection of short stories is an alarming excursion to a world populated by the suffering, the delusional and the criminally insane. It contains tales of ingenious cruelty and sudden death in which menace and hilarity go hand in hand.

'A very funny book...in the best traditions of the last few decades of British comedy...I can't recommend this enough'
Time Out

'A collection of slick thrills, arch references and cunning gags'
Independent on Sunday

VINTAGE BOOKS
London

BY DAVID L. HAYLES
ALSO AVAILABLE FROM VINTAGE

☐ **The Suicide Kit**   0099431823   £6.99
